"Don't p... Maggie."

Neil continued. "I'm not the fool I once was. Believe me, I'm still tempted to send you back where you belong."

Maggie wrapped the towel about her and took a deep breath. "Lindsey, too?" she asked tautly, and he scowled at her defiant face.

"Why not?" he said carelessly.

"Because she's your daughter," retorted Maggie harshly.

"Is she?" he asked. "How do I know that some other man's not her father?"

Maggie gulped. "That's a foul thing to say."

"But not unwarranted," he declared. "You lied to me before, Maggie."

She shook her head helplessly. "If you'd let me explain..."

"Later," he said wearily now. "Luke's waiting for his supper. I suggest you put some clothes on and join us."

ANNE MATHER began writing when she was a child, progressing through torrid teenage romances to the kind of adult romances she likes to read. She's married, with two children, and she lives in the north of England. After writing, she enjoys reading, driving, and traveling to different places to find settings for new novels. She considers herself very lucky to do something that she not only enjoys, but also gets paid for.

Books by Anne Mather

HARLEQUIN PRESENTS

Anne Mather

Long Night's Loving

Harlequin Books

TORONTO • NEW YORK • LONDON
AMSTERDAM • PARIS • SYDNEY • HAMBURG
STOCKHOLM • ATHENS • TOKYO • MILAN
MADRID • WARSAW • BUDAPEST • AUCKLAND

ISBN 0-373-11887-2

LONG NIGHT'S LOVING

First North American Publication 1997.

Copyright © 1997 by Anne Mather.

This edition published by arrangement with Harlequin Books S.A.

Printed in U.S.A.

CHAPTER ONE

MAGGIE got off the train at Newcastle.

The icy wind hit her as soon as she emerged from the insulated warmth of the carriage, and she shivered, in spite of the long cashmere coat and fur-lined boots she was wearing.

The shiver was more than just a reaction to the elements, however. For the past three hours she had felt a curious kind of detachment within the bustling community of the train. She'd almost been able to enjoy the journey, despite her apprehension at its completion. For a while, at least, she had put the reasons for making it aside, allowing herself the luxury of putting her fears on hold.

Still, now that she had actually made the decision to approach Neil, she was feeling a certain amount of relief. She hadn't realised it, but she had been fighting the idea for so long, she was weary, and, giving in to what he would probably see as a sign of weakness, she had surrendered the independence she had once considered so important.

Of course, he could refuse to help her. To help Lindsey, she amended firmly, even though she knew she was here as much for herself as for her daughter. Lindsey's attitude in recent weeks had left her feeling helpless, and curiously lost. Lindsey seemed to blame her for everything, and the knowledge that she could no longer get through to the girl was more than she could take.

Maggie knew her daughter had taken her parents' divorce badly, and for that she had no one to blame but herself. But it wasn't her fault that Lindsey refused to discuss the present situation with her, and ignored her mother's wishes out of hand.

Now, looking hopefully round the platform, she was not really surprised that there was no sign of Neil, or Luke Parry. She hadn't really expected her ex-husband would take the time to come and meet her, but she had hoped that Luke might have made the trip. She pulled a wry face. But then, she reflected, why should Neil make this easy for her? If past experience was anything to go by, she was probably wasting her time—and his.

She sighed. It wasn't the first time she had come here, hoping for Neil's understanding. When he'd first told her he was getting a divorce, she had flown up from London then, desperate to explain what had happened, but Neil wouldn't listen to her. He was not a man who forgave easily, she had discovered, and she had no reason to believe he had changed since. Her only justification for making this trip was that in this instance he had agreed to see her, and that only after she had mentioned Lindsey's name, and the fact that it was their daughter and not herself she wanted to discuss.

It was a cold grey day. It wasn't the time of year to come this far north and she thought, with a momentary trace of wistfulness, of the winters they had once spent in Antigua or St. Lucia. She hadn't appreciated it then. She'd been too young and foolish to be grateful for the advantages Neil's success had given her. She'd taken everything for granted, not least that as Neil's wife she was given the kind of respect she had neither earned nor warranted.

There were taxis waiting, their windows steamed by the breath of their idling drivers. She wondered how much it would cost to take a taxi to Bellthorpe. It used to cost quite a lot five years ago, and what with the rising cost of petrol, and inflation...

The alternative was to take a bus, and she seemed to remember the coach station was off Percy Street. Which meant quite a walk lugging her belongings. She didn't have a suitcase—she wouldn't have presumed to look as if she expected to stay the night—but she did have a canvas hold-all, and she knew from experience how heavy it could feel after she'd carried it some distance.

There was a canopy outside the station, enabling travellers to get in and out of their cars without the inconvenience of getting wet. But it didn't prevent the wind from sweeping up from the river, and Maggie cast a doubtful look at the waiting cabs.

At last deciding she couldn't stand here indefinitely, she moved with some reluctance to the front of the queue of cars. The taxi occupying the pole position wasn't the one she'd have chosen, if she'd had the chance, but she knew better than to approach one of the other drivers, and have him accused of jumping the queue.

But, as she bent to ask the driver how much he'd charge to take her the twenty or so miles to Bellthorpe, another car accelerated into first place. Not a taxi this time, but a mud-splattered Range Rover, with a scowling, dark-haired man at the wheel.

'Mags!'

Neil's curt voice arrested her, and she turned, not without a quiver of anticipation, to see her ex-husband thrusting open the passenger door from inside. The irritation she used to feel at his diminution of her name was absent, however. She was so relieved to see him; so relieved that she wouldn't have to spend more of her hard-earned cash on a taxi fare.

'Sorry I'm late,' he said, exchanging a challenging look with the driver of the cab, who had suddenly lost a passenger. 'Get in,' he added, as if the other man's feelings mattered to him, but she knew of old that however resentful the driver might be he'd get no satisfaction from Neil.

'Thanks.'

Because of the tightness of her skirt, Maggie scrambled without much dignity into the car. God, she thought, with a feeling of impatience at her ungainly entry. Had Neil brought this vehicle deliberately? It was worse than getting on a bus.

Once she was inside, however, she had to admit it was comfortable. And roomy; and it was warm, which was something she appreciated. She thrust her holdall into the back and slammed her door securely. Only then did she glance at her ex-husband as he concentrated on rejoining the stream of traffic heading towards Elswick.

It was a nerve-racking moment. It was almost five years since she'd seen him, and somehow she'd expected he would have changed. The fact that, apart from a certain narrowing of his features, he hadn't was hardly reassuring. He was obviously living his life quite happily, without worrying about her—or Lindsey—at all.

A few specks of rain hit the windscreen and because the silence in the car was getting to her Maggie gestured towards the darkening sky. 'Typical,' she said. 'It's raining. It always rains when I come to Newcastle.'

'Then it's just as well the reservoirs don't depend on you for their existence,' remarked Neil drily. 'We'd have had a drought.'

Maggie's breath surged from her lungs. 'Is that supposed to mean something?' she demanded, hurt by his sarcasm, and Neil sighed.

'It was supposed to be a joke,' he said shortly, and without much sympathy. 'Did you have a pleasant journey? Perhaps we can talk about that without you getting in a snit.'

'I'm not in a snit.' Maggie took a defensive breath, calming herself. 'And—yes, I had a very pleasant journey. The train wasn't full, and it was on time.'

'Unlike me?' suggested Neil, with another wry look in her direction, and Maggie wondered if it was his intention to provoke her.

'As you say,' she answered, without rising to his bait. 'But that wasn't what I meant either. I—wasn't sure you'd meet me.'

'As a matter of fact, I didn't intend to,' said Neil, his hands drawing her attention against her will. He had attractive hands, long-fingered and artistic. 'Luke was going to meet you, but he twisted his knee this morning, so he had to cry off.'

'I'm sorry.' Maggie meant it. For all he was Neil's ally, not hers, she had always had a soft spot for Luke Parry. He and Neil had grown up together in Byker, and when Neil had formed his first band Luke had played keyboard. But that was many years ago now, long before Neil had struck out on his own. In later years, Luke had been his road manager, before disillusionment—and the problems she and he were having—had driven Neil back to Tyneside. Luke was his assistant now, and part-time secretary. Their friendship had withstood the test of time.

'No sweat,' Neil declared now, switching on the wipers to clear the screen. 'He probably won't mention it, but he's having some trouble with his hip. He had a motorcycle accident about two years ago, and none of us are as young as we were.'

'Luke's not old!'

'He's nearly forty, the same as me,' observed Neil carelessly. 'We're not kids any more, Maggie. We're almost middle-aged.' His lips twisted. 'Not that I've forgotten I can give you a few years.'

Maggie said nothing, concentrating on the wet slick of the road ahead instead of giving in to the urge to look at him again. Almost forty, she thought, which meant she was almost thirty-six. As he'd said, they weren't kids any more. So why did she feel so immature suddenly?

'Are you well?' she asked, aware of the muscled length of his thigh, taut beneath its worn covering of denim. Almost involuntarily she was aware that he was wearing a loose knitted sweater beneath his leather jacket, long boots on his feet, manipulating the controls.

'Fine,' he answered briefly. 'And you?'

'Fine,' she mimicked, without thinking. 'Um—is Mrs Benson still at the house?'

'No. She retired,' he responded, and Maggie felt an enormous sense of relief. The elderly housekeeper had always resented her for being a 'Southerner', and it was one less person for her to confront.

'So—so who's looking after you now?' she asked, and he cast her an amused look.

'Do you really care?' he asked, his dark eyes bright with unconscious irony. 'As I remember it, my welfare was never high on your list of priorities, not even when we were living together.'

'That's not true!'

Her denial was instinctive, but although she stared at him indignantly he turned his attention back to the road. It was getting dark, so she could hardly blame him for that, but it was infuriating that he should still be able to wound her after all this time.

While she absorbed this evidence of her own weakness, they negotiated the southern outskirts of the city, and turned west onto the road for Carlisle. Signs indicating the nearness of the Roman Wall loomed at frequent intervals, and the announcement that this was 'Catherine Cookson Country' was vaguely familiar.

But it was a bleak landscape in the fading light of a January afternoon. Skeletal trees bent into the wind, and the few animals that had braved the weather huddled together in the corners of the fields, seeking shelter. It was the time of year, of course, but she felt a sense of isolation. Perhaps she'd lived too long in London, as Neil used to say. Perhaps she was afraid of the silence of her thoughts.

At least it wasn't snowing, she thought gratefully, and it could have been. These border counties of England saw more than their fair share of severe winter weather. She wondered what she'd have done if it had been snowing. Bellthorpe had been known to be cut off in the past.

'How's Lindsey?'

His question was sudden, if not unexpected. But Maggie didn't want to get into their daughter's problems in the car. No, she and Neil had to talk—it was why she was here, for heaven's sake—and she wanted to be able to see his face when she told him. She had no intention of revealing her reasons for coming here in the anonymous shadows of the vehicle.

So, 'She's OK,' she replied, after a moment's consideration. 'Um—did you have a good Christmas? I seem to remember there was snow in your part of the country, wasn't there? White Christmases are so rare these days. I imagine it was quite—'

'What do you want, Maggie?'

His curt interruption caught her unawares, and for a moment she could only look blankly in his direction.

'Well, you didn't come here to discuss the weather, did you?' he countered, dark eyebrows raised in an interrogatory stare. 'Come on, Maggie, spit it out, why don't you? It will save us from all this meaningless chatter.'

Maggie took a steadying breath. 'I see you haven't changed,' she remarked, without answering him. 'Patience was never your strong suit.'

'And candour was never yours,' he retorted harshly, accelerating to pass another car. 'I'm tired of your secrets, Maggie. You're here, aren't you? At least have the decency to get to the point.'

Maggie refused to be stampeded. 'When I phoned, you said I could spend the night.'

'That doesn't mean I'm prepared to entertain you,' replied Neil, in a controlled voice. 'Luke is at the house. It may be some time before we can talk privately. If what you have to say concerns Lindsey I'd rather know what it is now.'

Maggie couldn't disguise her sudden intake of breath. 'Why are you so aggressive?' she protested.

'Because of the way you avoided answering me before,' he replied in a weary tone. 'Don't be tiresome, Mags, I'm not an idiot. What's the matter with her? Has she got herself pregnant?'

Maggie gasped. 'No!'

But she half wished she had. She might have been able to cope with an unwanted pregnancy. She wouldn't have had to approach Neil for a start.

'What, then?'

He was slowing now, indicating that he was turning right at the next junction, turning onto the narrower road that led first to Chollerford, and then on, into the less populated heart of Northumberland.

Maggie turned to look out of the window. 'I'd rather not discuss it in the car.'

'Why not?'

'Because I wouldn't.' She was feeling indignant now. 'What's the matter, Neil? Don't you want to take me to the house?'

'Not particularly,' he answered, almost cruelly, and it took an enormous effort of will-power not to demand he take her back to the station right away. She should never have come here, she thought. She should have realised how he would regard it. She'd sworn she'd never ask him for anything ever again, and she hated going back on her word.

'Well, at least I know where I stand,' she said at last, managing to conceal the anguish his words had given her. 'But I'm sorry. I have no intention of discussing your daughter at this moment. If you hadn't wanted to accommodate me, you should have booked me a room at a hotel.'

'Yes, I should,' he remarked, pausing at the traffic lights at Chollerford Bridge. 'How about here?' He gestured towards the lights of the George Hotel that stood at the crossroads. 'You could always get a taxi back to town.'

For a moment, she thought he meant it, and her face turned towards his in sudden anxiety. But when the lights changed, and he accelerated over the bridge, he didn't turn into the hotel yard, and she realised he had only been baiting her again. It seemed he had accepted that, however compromised he might feel, he had to take her to Bellthorpe, to the dower house he'd purchased on the Haversham estate.

It was full dark by the time they reached Bellthorpe, and the rain that had accompanied them from Newcastle was now a steady downpour. Yet, for all that, there were a few people about in the village, and the windows of the post office and general stores cast a shaft of yellowish light across the road.

When Neil had first bought the house here, Maggie had thought he was crazy. When would he ever find the time to live here? she'd asked. His work was in London. The recording studios were there.

Of course she hadn't realised then that Neil was planning on giving up his recording career, that his ambition had changed to one of writing music instead of performing it. She'd been so wrapped up in creating her own identity, she had not noticed he was having a crisis with his. She'd been so selfish—she could admit it now—and stupid. But she doubted Neil would believe her if she said so.

The Haversham estate extended almost to the outskirts of the village. When Neil had moved here from the house they had owned in Buckinghamshire—how many years ago? Six? Seven?—the estate had been owned by an elderly recluse called Sarah Cavendish, and Maggie remembered making a rather poor joke about *Great Expectations*, and what a pity it was that Miss Cavendish hadn't been called Haversham, too. She'd even made fun of Neil, by suggesting that if he stayed here long enough people would forget him, as well. But, of course, they never had...

The house Neil had bought had once been occupied by the various widows of the family who'd owned the estate in the nineteenth century, when the eldest son inherited his father's position in the community. But it was years since it had been used for its original purpose, and when Neil had bought the property it had been in an appalling state of repair. The last tenant had been a farm labourer, who had left before the last war, and Maggie had considered Neil's offer ludicrous, for a house that, in her opinion, wanted pulling down.

Of course, she had had to eat her words. Time—and money—had worked wonders, and by the time it was ready for habitation even she had had to agree that it had become a home to be proud of. The trouble was, she had still wanted to live near London, and no house in Northumberland, however luxurious, could compensate her for that.

She remembered they had had their own entrance to the estate. The dower house was situated some distance from Haversham House itself, and it had been convenient, not just for Neil but for Miss Cavendish as well, for them to use an alternative way in. Consequently, she was surprised when Neil slowed at the tall iron gates that guarded the main entrance, and she cast him a puzzled look as they turned into the entry.

But before she could say anything a man emerged from the conical-roofed lodge that stood just inside the gates, and with some ceremony threw the gates wide for them to drive through.

'Evening, Mr Jordan,' he said as Neil lowered his window to thank him. He shielded his eyes against the downpour, and looked at Neil with evident respect. 'I found that break in the fence, like you said, and I've had a word with Ben Armstrong's man just this afternoon.'

'Great.' Maggie got the impression Neil would have avoided this discussion if he could. 'I'll talk to you about it tomorrow, Frank. You get on in out of this rain.'

'Yes, sir.' The man pulled a wry face. 'At least it's better than the snow. Did you hear the forecast? They say there's a depression coming over from the continent.'

'No, I didn't hear that.' Maggie could hear the controlled patience in Neil's voice. 'Goodnight, Frank. Give my regards to Rachel.'

'I will.'

The man stood back, and Neil accelerated away along the drive. In the wing mirror on her side of the car, Maggie could see the lodge-keeper closing the gates behind them, and her brows drew together in an expression of disbelief.

'You know,' she said, trying to sound casual, 'if I didn't know better, I'd say that man was treating you like his employer.' She paused. 'Are you?'

Neil's eyes were glued to the streaming track illuminated by the headlights. 'Am I what?' he asked, but she knew he was only avoiding the question.

'His employer,' she repeated tightly. 'Dear God, Neil, do you own the whole estate?'

'And if I do?'

Her lips parted. 'You never told me!'

'Why should I? What I do has nothing to do with you.'

There was an edge to his voice now, but she didn't notice it. 'So what happened to Miss Cavendish? Did you force her to leave, too?'

Neil cast her a look that she could only sense in the dim light from the dashboard, but the temperature in the vehicle had dropped several degrees. 'She died,' he said coldly. 'People do, when they get old. Don't judge everyone by your standards, Maggie. Miss Cavendish had done nothing wrong.'

Maggie's jaw felt tight. 'And I had?'

'Well, hadn't you?' he queried, with an irritating trace of contempt in his voice. He heaved a sigh. 'I think it's best if we don't discuss the past, don't you, Maggie? We said all there was to say five years ago. There's not much point in rehashing old scores now.'

Maggie said nothing. She was already regretting coming here, giving Neil the right to treat her as he liked. She didn't want to be beholden to him; she didn't want to ask him for anything. If it weren't for Lindsey she wouldn't be here. Couldn't he at least give her the benefit of the doubt?

There were bushes edging the drive, dripping with water at present, a far cry from the riot of colour they presented in spring. When she'd first seen them, Neil had told her they were rhododendrons, and even she had had to admit that their lush blooms of yellow and red and purple were magnificent. On a clear day, they had provided a useful screen for the house, but tonight there was no need of any cultivated concealment.

Nevertheless, when they emerged from the tall banks of greenery onto the open forecourt before the house Maggie couldn't deny a sudden feeling of liberation. The front of the house was illuminated, and the light spread over the blocked paving of the courtyard. She could see now that the stagnant pool that had once provided a centre-piece was gone, and in its place a fountain, in the shape of a nymph playing coyly in the water, added its rhythm to the falling rain.

Outwardly, the house itself was little changed. There was still greenery growing over its walls, and the tall mullioned windows still flanked the double doors with their pedimented portico. But instead of being dark many of the windows were lit, and in the late afternoon gloom it had an undeniable appeal.

Maggie drew her lower lip between her teeth. She thought she understood why Neil had been reluctant to bring her here. The dower house—well, they had once shared that, if only infrequently, but this place could hold no memories for him. It must have been deliberate, a desire to move into a place in which she had played no part? Or had he always intended to move here, once old Miss Cavendish had gone?

The Range Rover stopped, and as if on cue the doors of the house opened, and a man appeared in the aperture. He was heavier than she remembered, but no less recognisable, and she cast a glance at Neil, as if waiting for his permission to alight.

'As you can see, Luke is looking forward to meeting you,' he remarked without expression. He opened his door. 'You'd better run. This is the kind of rain that can soak you through in seconds.'

Maggie knew a moment's panic. 'Neil—'

'Go on,' he said, rather more harshly. 'He's waiting. If you hesitate any longer, he'll think there's something wrong.'

Maggie's lips tightened. 'And isn't there?'

'Not as far as I'm concerned,' remarked her ex-husband coolly. 'I've got your bag. Go ahead.'

CHAPTER TWO

MAGGIE paced restlessly about the bedroom, wondering when Neil was going to find the time to talk to her. Since they had arrived at the house, he had become frustratingly elusive, and it had been left to Luke Parry to make her feel at home.

Well, perhaps not that, she conceded, admitting that even Luke—dear Luke—had found it difficult to treat her as if nothing untoward had happened. It was five years for all of them, after all, and there was no denying that, however friendly he appeared, in any argument between them he would always take Neil's side.

Which was only as it should be, she supposed. What had happened between her and Neil would have stretched any bonds of friendship between herself and Luke, and he was unlikely to forget how much he owed his friend and employer.

Nevertheless, he had eased the awkwardness of her arrival. When Neil had stood back to allow her to precede him into the house, it had been Luke who had taken her hands and drawn her into the warmth of the firelit entrance hall, who had helped her out of her coat, and handed it to the round dumpling of a woman who she had later learned was Mrs Fenwick, Neil's new housekeeper.

'Maggie,' he'd said, gazing at her in his old approving way, as if he couldn't see the dark rings that underlined her eyes, or the traces of grey in her ash-blonde hair. 'Beautiful, as always. How do you do it?'

'By hypnotising the beholder,' she replied, with a wry glance over her shoulder. But Neil hadn't followed them into the spacious drawing room that opened off the hall, so he hadn't heard what Luke had said. Instead, she could hear his voice as he spoke to Mrs Fenwick, and although she couldn't hear every word she heard enough to know he was telling the woman that she would be spending the night.

'I don't think that's true,' declared Luke, indicating that she should seat herself in front of yet another log fire. Although the house was obviously centrally heated, the open fires created an atmosphere of warmth and comfort in the huge, high-ceilinged rooms. Rooms which had been expertly designed and renovated, so that Maggie's vision of cobwebs and crumbling plaster was banished for ever. 'How are you, Maggie? It's been a long time.'

It was only as Luke lowered himself with rather more care than usual onto the teal-green velvet sofa beside her that Maggie remembered what Neil had told her about him twisting his knee. He had made such a good job of hiding it up until that point, but bending it was obviously painful and Maggie felt a sense of shame.

'I'm fine,' she responded. 'How about you? Neil told me you'd twisted your knee. And that you'd had a motorcycle accident.'

'Neil should mind his own business,' declared Luke firmly, but there was no real censure in his voice. 'Believe it or not, I twisted my knee getting down from Sinbad. Oh—' he grinned at her puzzled expression '—he's the old hunter Neil keeps in the stables.'

Maggie's brows arched. 'You ride?'

'Yeah.' He grinned. 'Amazing, isn't it? Ten years ago, I wouldn't have known one end of a horse from the other.' He grimaced. 'But Neil is the biggest landowner hereabouts, and it's not always possible to reach every part of the estate in the four-by-four.'

'I see.' Maggie shook her head, trying to picture it. 'Neil rides too?'

'Oh, sure.' Luke's pale, still boyish features were a little ruddy now with embarrassment. 'Things have changed around here since Miss Cavendish died. No offence to you, Mags, but I think Neil's beginning to enjoy life again.'

Maggie managed a smile, but it took an effort. Yet it was what she wanted, wasn't it? she asked herself. The past—

well, the past was water under the bridge now, as they say, and whatever resentments Neil might still be nurturing towards her she was glad that she apparently hadn't ruined his life.

'That's good,' she said, albeit a little tensely, and determinedly turned her attention to the beautifully appointed room.

However doubtful she might have been about Neil's decision to move into the house, it was obvious that someone with taste had done the renovations. She refused to speculate how much money Neil must have spent, or why he had felt the need to buy a larger property. Nevertheless, it crossed her mind that the rug alone must have cost a small fortune, and what use she could have made of such a sum when her business had started to flag.

She drew a breath. How things had changed. When she'd first met Neil, he'd regarded her parents' modest semi with some admiration. He'd been brought up in a terraced house near the docks. Abandoned by his mother, he'd been raised by elderly grandparents, and he freely admitted he'd run wild when he was a teenager. But a spell in the army, and the opportunity to learn a musical instrument, had been the making of him, and pretty soon his ability both to write and perform his own music had been noticed.

Neil himself had always been essentially modest about his own achievements, which was another reason why he had become so successful. He could communicate with young people, and they could identify with him, and his pop career had gone from strength to strength...

'How's Lindsey?'

There it was. That question again, and this time no reason not to answer Luke. 'Oh—she's OK,' she replied, smooth- ing the fabric of her skirt along the thigh. She glanced towards the door. 'Where's Neil gone?'

'To arrange for some tea, I should think,' declared Luke, leaning towards the fire and jabbing at a precariously balanced log with his boot. 'Unless you'd prefer something stronger.' He gestured towards the cabinet behind him. 'Scotch, perhaps? Or a sherry?'

'Tea will be fine.'

Her response was less than enthusiastic, but she hadn't bargained on this long tête-à-tête with Luke. But it was typical of Neil to attempt to turn the tables on her. He must know she wouldn't have come all this way unless it was something serious. Just because she'd refused to discuss her problems in the car, he was choosing to keep her waiting.

'Did you have a good journey?'

Luke was speaking again, and, realising that she couldn't blame him for Neil's shortcomings, Maggie nodded. 'It was quite a novelty,' she said. 'It's ages since I've travelled on a train.'

'You could have flown up,' Luke pointed out, inadvertently putting his finger on something she preferred not to discuss. How could she explain that she'd needed the time the train took to cover the miles to gather her composure? A flight would have been too quick. It was important that she maintain the fiction that there was a huge physical distance between them.

'I—'

'Maggie doesn't really like planes. Don't you remember?'

While she had been struggling to come up with a suitable answer, Neil had entered the room behind them. He had shed his jacket, and now he walked across to prop one foot on the fender. It enabled her to take her first real look at him, and despite all her fine resolutions her stomach clenched.

It wasn't fair, she thought. She had changed. She knew she had. She had lines where she had never had lines before, and although she wasn't fat her waistline was a couple of inches thicker than it used to be. But Neil had barely changed at all. He was still tall, still lean, still moved with the unconscious grace of an athlete, and his raw-boned, angular features still possessed their addictive charm.

He was not a handsome man, but then, Maggie had never been attracted to men who were simply good-looking. The smooth-chested hunks she'd come into contact with in the course of her work had usually proved to have brawn, but no brains, whereas, for all his chequered upbringing, Neil's wit was as sharp as a knife.

Which was why, when he draped his elbow on the black marble mantel and looked down at her with dark, mocking eyes, she found herself incapable of parrying his remarks as she should. Dear God, she thought, looking down at her hands in sudden horrified confusion, he shouldn't still be able to disconcert her, but he did. She had been apprehensive of seeing him again, it was true, but she hadn't imagined the emotional upheaval it would cause her.

'Oh, yeah.' To her relief, Luke was answering him, giving her a few moments to collect herself. 'I'd forgotten,' he was saying. 'But it is some time since I've seen her. In any case, she overcame it. Isn't that right, Mags?'

Mags!

Maggie steeled herself against the urge to scream at him—at both of them—that that was not her name, but she knew it was just a reaction to the way she was feeling. She had to come to terms with the fact that the way Neil looked should not concern her. She wasn't an impressionable girl any more, and Neil wasn't interested in her body.

The reappearance of the housekeeper came as a welcome relief. The woman came bustling in, carrying a tray containing tea, shortbread biscuits and thickly buttered scones. She set the tray on the square lacquered table that stood between the sofa Maggie and Luke were occupying and its twin which stood opposite, and then straightened to give her employer a beaming smile.

'Will you be wanting anything else, Mr Jordan?' she asked, and Neil shook his head.

'This is fine, Mrs Fenwick,' he said. 'And by the way, this is Miss—I beg your pardon—*Ms* Freeman. As I said before, she'll be staying until tomorrow, and I know you'll make her welcome.'

'I'm very pleased to meet you, Ms Freeman,' declared the housekeeper cheerfully, and Maggie was forced to give her an answering smile.

'And I you, Mrs Fenwick,' she said, flushing with indignation at Neil's introduction. And, although it wasn't a question she would normally have asked, she added, 'Have you been at Haversham long?'

'About two years, Ms Freeman,' Mrs Fenwick replied,

apparently seeing nothing wrong with the enquiry. 'I came to work for Mr Jordan when he moved here from the old dower house.'

'Did you?'

Maggie's eyes flicked over her ex-husband's face, registering the irritation he was feeling at her curiosity. But at least she knew how long Neil had lived in this house now, which was something she'd have been loath to ask him.

'Well...' As if sensing that her employer didn't approve of her chattering with his guest, Mrs Fenwick smiled again and made for the door. 'I'll let you get your tea. Supper's at eight o'clock, Ms Freeman. But I expect Mr Jordan will tell you about that.'

'Thank you.'

Maggie was almost sorry the woman had gone, not least because Neil was now glowering at her with undisguised impatience. 'If you wanted to know how long I'd lived here, you should have asked me,' he declared tersely. 'Mrs Fenwick isn't here to satisfy your morbid interest in my affairs.'

Aware of Luke's discomfort, Maggie didn't respond as she might have done. 'It's not a morbid interest,' she denied, making an effort to speak politely. 'I just didn't remember Lindsey mentioning the fact that you'd moved.'

'As you've stopped Lindsey from coming to Haversham for the past two years, that's understandable,' retorted Neil, seating himself on the sofa opposite. He picked up the teapot. 'As you never liked being mother, shall I pour the tea?'

Maggie's nails dug into her palms. 'You have no right to say that,' she declared, deciding that if he wasn't prepared to respect Luke's feelings why should she?

'To say what?' Neil countered, and she took a quivering breath.

'That I never like being a mother!' she exclaimed, casting a helpless look in Luke's direction. 'And I've never stopped Lindsey from coming here. If she's stayed away, it's no fault of mine.'

Neil's eyes bored into hers. 'Are you saying it's mine?'

Maggie held up her head. 'I don't make accusations,' she replied, wishing she had never given him the chance to make her feel small. She glanced at Luke once again. 'I'm sorry,' she murmured. 'Neil always has to win every argument.'

Luke shifted a little uncomfortably. 'I wouldn't know,' he said, clearly unwilling to take sides. 'Um—why don't you have one of Mrs Fenwick's scones? She's a far better cook than Mrs Benson.'

Maggie felt as if she couldn't eat a thing. Her throat had closed up, and there was a sickly feeling in her stomach. 'Maybe later,' she said as Neil set a cup of tea on the table in front of her. 'I'm not very hungry right now.'

'Perhaps you'd like to rest for a while before supper,' suggested Luke, when Neil made no further comment. 'You'll find we have a wonderful view from the upstairs windows, although of course you won't be able to see anything tonight.'

'I—'

'That's a good idea,' declared Neil infuriatingly, leaning back against the soft velvet upholstery and taking a bite out of the warm scone he held in his hand. He licked a curl of butter from his lip with what Maggie knew was deliberate provocation. 'We're in no hurry to talk, are we, Maggie? I'm sure you'd appreciate some time to freshen up.'

Which was how she came to be pacing the bedroom she had been allotted now, facing the prospect of several more unproductive hours before Neil might deign to grant her his undivided attention. What was she supposed to do? He couldn't really expect her to rest when she had so much on her mind. But, of course, he'd say that he wasn't aware of that. After all, she hadn't confided in him.

She paused by the curtained windows, peering out, but all she could see was darkness. And raindrops, sliding continuously down the window-panes, dripping in eerie counterpoint from the trees.

She turned to look at the room behind her. It was a huge apartment, reaching up some twelve feet to the embossed ceiling, with a delicately sculpted cornice above the silk-lined walls. The bed dominated the room; large and four-posted, it nevertheless possessed a very comfortable mattress, as Maggie had already noted. The headboard was

carved, and the bedspread was made of peach-coloured bro-
cade, buttoned, to match the heavy curtains at the windows.

Beside the bed were two small cabinets, on which resided
a pair of peach-shaded lamps. There were flowers there,
too, a fragrant display of roses and chrysanthemums, whose
colours blended perfectly with the rest.

Two comfortable armchairs flanked a studded chest,
which Maggie guessed served the dual purpose of storage
compartment and table, while several other tables and an
exquisite French bureau gave the room an appealing sense
of intimacy.

She'd already discovered that there was an adjoining
dressing room, where guests could hang their clothes in
huge closets that could surely never be filled. And beyond
the dressing room she had her own spacious bathroom,
again furnished with every conceivable luxury.

Maggie sighed. She hadn't come here to admire Neil's
house, she thought frustratedly. She hadn't even known
he'd moved house, for heaven's sake, and although it was
all very beautiful it could mean nothing to her. But, the
way he was behaving, it might be tomorrow before she got
to speak to him alone, and she couldn't afford to stay away
too long.

She wondered what Lindsey was doing at this moment.
She knew better than to hope that her sister had had any
more success with her than she had. If Lindsey wanted to
see Mike Reynolds, she'd see him whether her mother and
her aunt wanted her to or not. She was completely uncon-
trollable, and Maggie was at her wits' end worrying about
her.

She took a deep breath and straightened away from the
window. Perhaps if she took a shower she'd feel better, she
thought. At least it would fill in some time, and although
she hadn't brought a change of outfit she had brought a
change of underwear. Or perhaps a bath, she considered
as she entered the bathroom. It was years since she'd had
a jacuzzi. Not since she and Neil had shared one in
Singapore...

But she didn't want to think of that now, didn't want to
think of Neil in any other way than the way he had behaved

earlier that afternoon. He'd expected her not to say anything, not to do anything to embarrass Luke. Yet he'd had no qualms about embarrassing her.

Pulling off her knitted waistcoat, her hands went to the buttoned fastening of her skirt. It fell to the floor, pooling about her ankles, and she stepped out of it to pull off her boots.

When she straightened, her eyes were irresistibly drawn to her reflection in the mirrored walls around her. God, she thought, this room did nothing for her ego. In her black skinny-rib sweater and pantihose, she was sure she looked every inch her age.

The sweater came off next, revealing the lacy contours of her bra. Her breasts were fuller these days, almost spilling out of the low-cut fabric, the V between them accentuated as she leant forward to turn on the taps.

Yet, for all she deplored the image the mirrors threw back at her, her eyes were drawn to them again and again. There was something almost sensual—almost sinful—in watching herself undress, and she was glad when the bath was full, and she could subside beneath the water.

And it was relaxing, amazingly so. Lying there, gazing up at the recessed lights above her head, she could feel much of the tension seeping out of her. She was here, wasn't she? she thought placidly. She had achieved her first objective. And she'd get to speak to Neil eventually, if she succeeded in avoiding the arguments he seemed to enjoy provoking.

Her eyes closed. Her head was propped on the rest at the end of the bath, made specially for just that purpose, and it was so delightful to submit to her own body's needs for a change. For weeks—months—all she'd thought of was Lindsey. Lindsey's needs, Lindsey's demands, Lindsey's future. It was heaven not to think of her daughter for a while, not to worry about what she was going to do...

'Don't you know it's dangerous to sleep in the bath?'

For a moment, Maggie didn't know where she was, and Neil's mocking voice didn't mean anything to her. She must have fallen asleep, she thought, because the water was beginning to feel cold, and she shivered as she forced herself to sit up.

And then she saw him, his lean frame reflected over and over in the mirrors all around her. He was propped against the open doorway that led into the adjoining dressing room, watching her with careless indifference as she struggled to hide her reaction from him.

'How did you get in?' she demanded, her hand reaching automatically for the facecloth to cover her puckered breasts, and then withdrawing again. Why should she be coy when he knew exactly what she was hiding? she decided tautly. Her breasts were one of her better features, even if they weren't as young and firm as they'd once been.

'How do you think?' Neil responded, and although his tone was just as careless she knew he'd noticed her body. His eyes had flickered, nothing more, but between her legs she felt a melting sensation that had nothing to do with why she was here.

'Then I suggest you get out again,' she said, realising that such feelings were exactly why she hadn't wanted to come. The last thing she wanted to do was let him see he could still disturb her. She must not let him get the upper hand, however emotional he made her feel.

Neil straightened, but he didn't turn away. He had changed his clothes, and she couldn't help noticing how well the cream collarless shirt and dark brown trousers suited him. The shirt was loose, but the trousers were tight, enveloping his long legs and powerful thighs like a second skin. Dear God, she thought, why had she ever thought Oliver Massey was attractive? Compared to Neil, he was just a cipher—a man she had trusted, and who had betrayed her in the cruellest kind of way.

'Believe it or not, but Luke was worried about you,' he said, raising one hand to support himself against the overhead lintel. 'It's nearly eight o'clock, or hadn't you noticed? He's waiting for you to join us downstairs.'

Maggie tightened her lips. 'And you're not?'

'Oh, I wouldn't say that.' Now there was no mistaking the studied appraisal he gave her. 'You're still a beautiful woman, Maggie. I'm sure you know that as well as me.

How many men have told you so in the last five years, I wonder? How many men have seen you as I'm seeing you now?'

Maggie bit back the urge to tell him. None! *None!* she wanted to cry, but admitting it would just be playing into his hands. 'Wouldn't you like to know?' she remarked instead, deliberately standing up so that he could see all of her. She reached for a towel and began to dry herself. 'What's the matter, Neil? Have you taken to being a voyeur in your old age?'

If she'd thought to disconcert him, she was sadly disappointed. 'Perhaps I have,' he answered, his dark eyes mirroring his contempt. 'When you're ready, we'll have supper. I'll tell Luke you're on your way, shall I?'

'If that's what you want to do,' said Maggie, hardly aware of what she was saying with those penetrating eyes stripping away everything, even her skin. She was naked before him, naked and vulnerable, but how vulnerable she hadn't realised until this moment.

'You have no idea what I want to do,' he retorted, just when she was thinking he was completely invincible, and she was trembling so badly, she could hardly step out of the bath. 'Just don't push your luck, Maggie. I'm not the fool I once was. Believe me, I'm still tempted to send you back where you belong.'

Maggie wrapped the towel about her, and took a deep breath. 'Lindsey, too?' she asked tautly, and he scowled at her defiant face.

'Why not?' he said carelessly.

'Because she's your daughter,' retorted Maggie harshly, and Neil's arm dropped to his side.

'Is she?' he asked, and Maggie stared at him disbelievingly. 'How do I know that some other man's not her father?'

Maggie gulped. 'That's a foul thing to say.'

'But not unwarranted,' he declared, turning so that his back was against the jamb. 'You've lied to me before, Maggie. Don't make me go into details. I'm fit to pay her bills, but little else, it seems.'

'That's not my fault!'

'So you say.'

'It's the truth.' Maggie shook her head helplessly. 'If you'd let me explain…'

'Later,' he said, wearily now. 'Luke's waiting for his supper. I suggest you put some clothes on and join us.'

CHAPTER THREE

MAGGIE wished she'd brought a change of clothes with her when she saw that Luke had put on a fresh shirt and tie, too. He got awkwardly to his feet as she walked into the drawing room fifteen minutes later, and she offered a rueful apology for being late.

'No sweat,' he averred, glancing at Neil, who was standing in his previous position on the hearth. 'Did you have a rest?'

Hardly, thought Maggie half-impatiently, her eyes seeking Neil's, as if for confirmation. Had he told Luke what had happened? She rather doubted it. She sighed. Of course. He wouldn't want to embarrass the other man.

'I had a bath,' she said, aware that Neil was watching her and wondering what he'd say if she told Luke he'd entered her bedroom without permission. More than that, he'd entered her bathroom, and shown no shame at the intrusion. He'd violated her privacy. No wonder he hadn't told his friend.

'Good idea,' approved Luke, totally unaware of the undercurrents in the room, or, if he was, making a valiant effort not to show it. 'I enjoy a shower as much as anyone, but nothing beats the comfort of a hot bath on a cold day.'

'Or night,' said Maggie, accepting the glass of sherry he offered her. She sipped it experimentally. 'Mmm, this is nice. Amontillado.'

'That's right.' Luke was pleased. 'I remember now. It's your favourite.'

'I don't recall Maggie having a favourite,' retorted Neil, spoiling the moment. 'Unless it was Scotch. I remember she was once very fond of that.'

Maggie refused to be provoked and, as if grateful for her forbearance, Luke urged her to sit down. He joined her on the sofa again, clearly glad to be off his injured leg, and Maggie contented herself with looking about the room.

Like the bedroom upstairs, the high ceiling gave it an added elegance. Tall Chinese cabinets were set against wine silk walls, with a proliferation of pictures in between. There were two pairs of end tables, adorned by either vases of flowers or in one case a Tiffany lamp, and beneath the long windows, swagged now with dark green velvet curtains, a grand piano stood, with its lid upraised. Maggie guessed that when the curtains were open the view from its matching stool must be quite impressive.

'Your bedroom's warm enough?' Luke persisted, obviously feeling an obligation to make their guest feel at home, and Maggie nodded.

'It's lovely,' she assured him, pressing her back against the cushions behind her, and Luke reached for his own glass of Scotch, residing on the table nearby.

'I suppose Lindsey's quite grown-up now,' he continued, and although Maggie refused to look in Neil's direction she sensed his close attention to her answer. She was tempted to change the subject, to see how he'd react. But she didn't.

'She's seventeen,' she agreed instead, taking refuge in her sherry. Then she asked, 'Do you ever see Barbara these days?'

She hadn't meant to embarrass him, but it was obvious she had. Luke and Barbara had got married soon after herself and Neil, but it had been apparent, right from the start, that it wasn't going to work. Maggie had had the suspicion that Luke had only got married to prove he could sustain a relationship, and by the time he'd realised his mistake Barbara was expecting twins.

The twins—both boys—must be nearly sixteen now, she thought—about a year younger than Lindsey. It would have been good if they'd lived close by. When she'd known them they'd been a lot like Luke: shy and sensitive. They might have had an improving influence on her daughter.

'Barbara's married again,' Luke conceded at last, and Maggie sensed that Neil resented her enquiry more than he did. She didn't know why. It wasn't as if Luke had been heartbroken when they'd split up. And he'd maintained a good relationship with his sons, which said a lot for his character.

'Would you like to come through?'

Mrs Fenwick's arrival eased the moment, and Luke got almost eagerly to his feet. His face twisted in pain as he jarred his knee, but it proved he welcomed the opportunity to avoid any further discussion of his affairs.

The dining room was across the hall, and Maggie took more notice of her surroundings. When she'd first entered the house, she'd allowed Luke's welcome to distract her, but now she was able to admire the Italian tiles beneath her feet, and the huge stone fireplace, above which the portrait of a seventeenth-century woman and her children took pride of place.

'That's Neil's Velazquez,' said Luke, seeing her interest and grateful for any diversion, however oblique.

'It's beautiful,' said Maggie, wondering when Neil had become such a connoisseur. Was that what this house had done to him? Turned him into a man she barely recognised?

The dining room was panelled in oak, with a long polished table that was presently set for only three. But, looking along its length, Maggie could quite believe it could seat at least twenty, and she wondered if her ex-husband often gave dinner parties.

If he did, that too was a change from his previous way of living. When they'd been together, he had deplored the parties given by his friends and colleagues in the music business—parties where drugs and alcohol had been freely available, and you weren't considered to be enjoying yourself unless you were high. Maggie hadn't liked them to begin with, but they had been a way of asserting her independence, and when things between them had become unpleasant she had gone on her own...

The food Mrs Fenwick served was superb, and quite endorsed Luke's assertion that she was a better cook than Mrs Benson. The previous housekeeper had served what she called 'good English food' but Maggie would have argued with that presumption. She was sure Mrs Benson's stodgy puddings and soggy vegetables would have turned a stronger stomach than hers.

They ate a creamy watercress mousse, saddle of lamb with new potatoes and green beans, and a fruit compote to finish. Nothing stodgy, nothing heavy, nothing to lie uncomfortably on the stomach when you retired. The whole meal was a delight, as was the freshly brewed coffee that followed, which was served back in the drawing room, in front of the fire.

In spite of her misgivings earlier, the conversation during the meal had not been stilted, even if they had stuck to uncontroversial issues. And, toasting her toes before the fire, Maggie reflected that they could be old friends—at least, that was the image an outsider might be forced to believe.

'Does—er—does Mrs Fenwick do everything?' she asked, accepting a second cup of coffee, and this time Neil chose to answer her himself.

'In a house this size?' he asked wryly. 'No, I don't think she could manage alone, even though she is very efficient. But she and her husband are the only members of staff who live on the premises.'

Maggie arched a dark brow. 'Her husband? The man we saw at the gatehouse when we arrived?'

'No.' Neil was patient. 'The man you saw was Frank Pitt. He works on the estate. Mrs Fenwick's husband is the gardener, and occasional chauffeur.'

'I see.'

Maggie was impressed. By her reckoning that was at least four people working directly for Neil, and goodness knew how many more in the stables and about the estate. Some of the land was tenanted, of course—she remembered that from when they had first come here—but it was obvious that Neil took his position seriously.

Her lips twisted. Neil had always known what he wanted out of life, whereas she had spent the past ten years trying to find her own identity. It had been different when she was younger. Then, just the fact that she was Neil's wife had been enough. When had she started being dissatisfied with that scenario? When had she begun to believe that life owed her a living too?

Luke finished his coffee, and set his cup back on the tray. 'Well—' he yawned, stretching his arms above his head '—I think I'm ready to call it a day.' He looked at Maggie. 'I expect I'll see you in the morning. I'll come over for breakfast, if it's all right with Neil?'

'Come over?' Maggie moistened lips that were suddenly dry. 'But I thought—' She broke off, and then began again. 'Don't you live in the house?'

'Not precisely,' said Luke, grinning. 'As a matter of fact, I have my own apartment over the garage. Oh, don't worry—' this as he saw her expression '—it's really very comfortable. You'll have to see it tomorrow. I'll give you a guided tour before you leave.'

Before she left.

Maggie managed a tight smile. 'Thanks.'

But she was still aware of a feeling of apprehension. Which was silly really, because she couldn't have expected any support from him. But she'd felt more relaxed knowing he was within calling distance. The knowledge that there'd only be herself and Neil in the house—discounting his other employees, of course—was rather daunting.

Yet why should that be so? she asked herself as Neil escorted the other man to the door. It wasn't as if they hadn't spent a good portion of their lives together, even if they had been seldom entirely on their own. It was the memory of that treacherous weakening she had felt in the bath that troubled her, she knew. The awareness that she wasn't as indifferent to him as she'd like to appear. She could think of nothing more embarrassing, more painful than allowing him to think she had some hidden agenda of her own in coming here.

She was aware that Neil had returned before he came round the sofa to resume his seat. She felt his presence the minute he appeared in the doorway, knew that he paused there for a moment, probably deliberately, assessing how he would handle her request.

Not that he knew what that request was—yet. But he must have guessed it was something serious, as she hadn't been willing to discuss it in the car. What was he thinking? she wondered. Was he speculating on how he would refuse her? Although she had made the journey, she wasn't totally optimistic, particularly after that crack he had made about Lindsey earlier.

'Would you like a drink?' he enquired, his hand hovering over the tray of bottles and decanters residing on a small table against the wall, and Maggie shook her head. She'd had sherry—and wine—and she needed her wits about her. Apart from not giving him another chance of criticising her lack of sobriety.

'Not for me,' she said, unable to prevent herself from shifting a little nervously in her seat. She wished he would just sit down and listen to her. She was tired of this game of cat-and-mouse, tired of bearing the burden she carried alone.

'You don't mind if I do?'

She shook her head again, biting hard on her lower lip to stop herself screaming. Her nerves felt as if they were stretched to breaking point, and she was pretty sure he knew it, too.

'OK.' At last, he seated himself across the table from her again, sitting forward on the sofa cushions, legs splayed, hands holding his glass of either Scotch or brandy suspended between them. 'How much?'

Maggie swallowed her chagrin. 'How much what?'

'Oh, please.' Neil heaved a weary sigh. 'How much is it going to cost me to get rid of you?'

Maggie could hardly speak now. 'Why, you—you—'

'Bastard?' he queried flatly. 'I sensed your feelings towards me in the car. Nevertheless, I think we should be honest with one another. There's nothing much else left between us. You implied that Lindsey's in some kind of trouble, so how much is it going to take to bail her out?'

Maggie pressed her lips together to prevent them from trembling. 'You think money can cure everything, don't you?'

'And you're going to tell me it can't?'

'Yes.' Maggie shook her head. 'If only it were that simple. Do you think I'd have come to you if all I needed was money?' Her lips quivered. 'I'd have mortgaged everything I owned before I asked you for a loan!'

Neil's eyes flickered. 'Then I don't see what else I can do,' he averred. 'Lindsey's too old for me to punish. I doubt she'd take any notice if I did.'

'Maybe. Maybe not.' Maggie permitted him a fleeting look from between her lashes. 'I suppose we haven't set her a very good example.'

'Speak for yourself,' retorted Neil sharply. 'I've done nothing to be ashamed of, and don't you forget it.' He halted, as if realising they'd get nowhere by sniping at each other. 'So what is it? What's she done? What kind of trouble is she in?'

'She says she's in love with Mike Reynolds.'

'You're crazy!'

She'd caught his attention now, and Maggie allowed herself a moment's satisfaction at his furious reaction. Then, 'I wish I were,' she declared offhandedly. 'Now do you see why I had to come?'

Neil stared at her in horror. 'But Reynolds is my age!'

'Do you think I don't know that?'

'So what the hell is he doing playing around with someone who's little more than a kid?'

'Lindsey's seventeen,' Maggie reminded him gently. 'She wouldn't appreciate your calling her a schoolgirl. These last two years—well, she's grown up. I can't tell her what to do any more.' She paused. 'If I ever could.'

'Have you tried?'

That caught her on the raw. 'Of course I've tried. Do you think I want her involved with him?'

'I don't know what you want,' said Neil dourly, getting up from his seat and pacing restlessly about the room. 'I sometimes think I never knew you at all.'

'That's not true!'

'Isn't it?' He shrugged his shoulders, clearly using her as an outlet for his frustration. 'You've never given a damn for anyone but yourself. Is it any wonder Lindsey's screwed up now?'

Maggie chose not to answer that, and then stiffened when Neil came back to where she was sitting. But all he did was pick up his glass and empty it, returning to the tray to pour himself another. Having mixed it to his liking, he turned back to her again, swallowing a mouthful, and then crossing his arms at his waist.

'So, what am I supposed to do about it? As I've already said, I don't have any magic potion. I doubt if she'd even want to hear what I had to say.'

'She might.' Maggie composed herself. 'It's worth a try, anyway. If not...' she paused '...Mike has his own agenda. He says he'll drop Lindsey if you agree to make another album.'

'What?'

Maggie drew an uneven breath. 'I think you heard what I said.'

'OK, I heard,' he bit out savagely, 'but you don't seriously expect me to do it? I gave up performing seven years ago, and I don't intend to make a come-back, for you or anyone else.'

'Or Lindsey?' ventured Maggie tautly, and Neil paused behind the sofa opposite to give her a killing look.

'Or Lindsey,' he snarled. 'Goddammit, what are you trying to do to me? Why the hell should I disrupt my life for someone I hardly know?'

'Someone you hardly know?' Maggie could sit still no longer. She sprang to her feet to gaze angrily at him. 'Until she was twelve, there was no one else in her life but you!'

'Because you had no time for her.'

'No. Because she idolised you, and you know it. For pity's sake, don't deny her identity, Neil. If you haven't seen her recently, that's as much your fault as hers.'

'How is it?' Neil scowled. 'I've invited her here—several times. If she's chosen not to come, that's not my fault.'

'She's a teenager, Neil,' retorted Maggie wearily. 'Isn't it natural that she finds there's more to do in London?'

'Are we talking about Reynolds here?'

'No, we're not.' Maggie sighed. 'That's a fairly recent aberration. But she has friends—boyfriends, even—and a fairly active social life. She told me that the last time she came here you were working most of the time.'

A trace of colour entered Neil's face now. 'I didn't real-

ise she was bored,' he said defensively. 'Luke took her
riding. They hired hacks from the local riding school in
those days. She probably told you. And I believe he took
her to the speedway stadium at Gateshead. When she was
younger, she used to be keen on that.'

'She didn't come all this way just to spend time with
Luke,' Maggie pointed out steadily. 'She said she thought
you weren't really interested in what she did.'

'Oh, and I suppose you jumped on that as a reason for
keeping her away,' inserted Neil angrily. 'If she'd been
living at Haversham, she'd never have got involved with
the likes of Mike Reynolds, would she?'

Maggie stiffened. 'Do you expect me to answer that?'

'Well, it's true, isn't it? You never had any time for
Lindsey when we were together, but as soon as I suggested
I should have custody you did everything you could to stop
me seeing her.'

'That isn't true.' Maggie stared at him indignantly. 'You
know I've never stopped you seeing her whenever you
wanted.'

'But you wouldn't let her live with me.'

Maggie sighed. 'A girl needs her mother.'

'And it was another way to hurt me—isn't that nearer
the truth?'

'No.' Maggie bent her head. 'This is getting us nowhere.'

'I agree.' Neil finished his drink and went to pour himself
a third. Then, turning, he surveyed her with bitter eyes.
'Why should I help you now? You've never wanted my
help before.'

Maggie expelled her breath. 'No.'

Neil's jaw compressed. 'Why didn't you bring her with
you?'

Maggie shrugged. 'She wouldn't have come.'

'She wouldn't have come?' Neil stared at her. 'Why
didn't you make her? How the hell am I supposed to talk
some sense into her if she's in London and I'm here?'

'You could go—'

'To London?' Neil shook his head. 'No way.'

'Then I'm wasting my time,' said Maggie flatly. 'Because you'll never get her to come to Haversham. Haven't

you been listening to anything I've said? She thinks she's in love with Mike Reynolds, and he's the only person who can get through to her these days.'

'The hell he is.'

Maggie started towards the door. 'I'll say goodnight,' she said, making no attempt to repudiate his statement, but Neil muttered a savage oath before stepping deliberately into her path.

'Like hell you will,' he snarled. 'We haven't finished—not by a long way. Don't think you can walk out of here after dropping that bombshell and expect me to forget all about it!'

'I thought that was what you wanted to do.'

Maggie was forced to look up at him now—either that or appear afraid to do so. But it wasn't easy facing him, when he was so close she could feel the heat of his body, so near she could smell the scent of what she could now recognise as brandy on his breath.

'I never said that,' he retorted harshly, and her eyes dropped to the shadow of his beard already darkening his jaw. To his mouth, which at present expressed all his frustration, and which she had once known as intimately as her own.

A quiver went through her, and she forced herself to concentrate on what he was saying. 'You're going to help me?'

'We'll see.' Neil set his empty glass on a table, and flexed his fingers against his thighs. 'Why don't you come back and sit down and we'll talk about it?'

Maggie held up her head. 'If this is some sort of game...'

'It's not.'

Maggie hesitated, and with a muffled groan Neil turned her back into the room. 'Don't look at me like that,' he said grimly, prodding her towards the sofa. 'I've no intention of wasting my time—or yours.'

CHAPTER FOUR

NOT for the first time since she'd arrived at Haversham, Maggie wished she had something different to wear. Her skirt was creased, and the skinny-rib sweater had a wine stain, she noticed unhappily.

Still, she had no choice but to wear it—and the skirt, she conceded ruefully. This wasn't some fairy tale where, when she opened the wardrobes in her dressing room, she was suddenly confronted with a magical choice of clothes. Her cupboards were disappointingly empty. There wasn't even a change of shoes.

Not that she had expected any. When she and Neil had separated, someone had taken intense pleasure in packing up all her belongings and forwarding them to her London house. They'd even sent the half-empty shampoo bottles she'd left in the bathroom. As if ensuring that she never attempted to visit Neil again.

Neil.

Still dressed in only her slip and pantihose, Maggie sank down onto the stool before the mirrored dressing table and regarded her reflection without liking. Hazel eyes stared back at her, green in some lights, and presently full of scorn for herself, and for the reason why she had come here. She'd known, before she left London, that, whatever resentment she might still hold towards her ex-husband, what she was going to ask him was outrageous. She'd known he'd never agree to it, not after all these years of sequestration. It wasn't his problem. She'd made it hers when she'd accepted custody of their daughter. She couldn't expect him to feel the same responsibility for Lindsey that she did. He was right. He owed Lindsey nothing. Certainly

not the curtailment of his freedom, of the privacy he'd
sought so long to maintain.

Yet when he'd insisted on her postponing her going to
bed the night before she had known a brief spurt of expec-
tation. She couldn't think of any other reason why he might
want to delay her and, for all her feelings of guilt and cul-
pability, she had returned to her seat on the sofa, with the
first shreds of hope she'd felt in a long time.

She should have known better. She should have realised
that Lindsey's involvement with a man old enough to be
her father, and Neil's estranged agent to boot, was unlikely
to stir any but the most primitive feelings of resentment.
Oh, sure, Neil didn't like it, but throwing away his future
for it was something else. He might find some other way
to get back at Mike Reynolds for trying to blackmail him,
but as far as he was concerned she was to blame.

Maggie's lips trembled for a moment and, seeing it, she
pressed an impatient hand against her mouth. You fool! she
berated herself. You stupid fool! Did you have to lose what
little dignity you possessed? Did you have to let him see
how weak you were?

She sought blindly for her make-up case which was lying
on the glass tray in front of her. Pulling out a jar of moist-
urising foundation, she began to smooth it onto her face.
Her skin was still supple, but she could only see the incipi-
ent wrinkles. Why was it that men aged so much slower? It
wasn't fair that women should bear that as well as everything else.

The first inkling she had had that Neil had more than a
simple discussion in mind had come when, after getting
them both a brandy, he'd chosen to sit beside her on the
same sofa. Instead of removing himself to the comparative
distance of the other sofa, he'd chosen to stretch his length
beside her, his heels propped carelessly on the edge of the
polished table, his thigh depressing the cushion by her hip.

'So, tell me,' he said, supporting his head with his hands
linked at his nape, 'how did Lindsey meet a rat like Mike
Reynolds?'

Maggie endeavoured to appear unmoved by his prox-
imity. 'He—I—he already knew her.'

'As a baby,' he amended drily. 'Lindsey was only ten when Reynolds and I parted company.'

'I know that.'

'So?'

'So, all right.' Maggie sighed. 'She met him at a party given by the fashion wholesalers. They thought it would be fun, having some celebrities present.'

Neil looked at her out of the sides of his eyes. 'Mike Reynolds is a celebrity?' he said disbelievingly. 'Since when?'

'He has some celebrity clients,' said Maggie uncomfortably, far too aware of the intensity of his gaze. 'Not least yourself—at least, when you were working.'

Neil's mouth turned down. 'I haven't stopped working.'

'You know what I mean,' declared Maggie, sighing. 'Touring, doing gigs, appearing on *Top of the Pops*, that sort of thing.' She ignored his ironic stare, and hurried on impulsively, 'He still has several good bands on his books.'

'Has he? I wouldn't know.'

Neil's tone was dismissive, but Maggie didn't quite believe him. If she knew her ex-husband, he'd know exactly what Mike Reynolds was doing, and with whom. Since the man had cheated Neil out of more than a million pounds, she'd have expected him to be waiting for a chance to get even.

'So, to advertise that rubbishy little business of yours, you introduced *our* daughter to the jerk of the year!'

'No.' Maggie was defensive. 'And it's not a rubbishy little business. We have two shops now. We have one in Bournemouth, as well as the one in London.'

'"We?"' Neil arched dark brows. 'Is that the royal "we", or do I take it you've got another man in tow?'

'It's we as in myself and Jackie,' retorted Maggie hotly. 'You knew my sister was a partner. It was because of her that I opened the boutique in the first place.'

'I thought it was to—how did you put it?—find yourself? Or something equally unlikely,' said Neil mockingly. 'Well, have you found what you were looking for? Or are you still searching?' He grimaced. 'It's a hell of a way to live your life.'

Maggie felt the unexpected prick of tears behind her eyes now. 'You're a cruel devil, Neil,' she told him. 'You never could resist making fun of me.'

'Then why don't I find it amusing?' he enquired sardonically. 'Come on, Maggie. Tell me about Reynolds. And why you would allow that bastard to get near my daughter.'

Maggie managed to stop herself from commenting on his sudden wish to assume paternity, and replied, 'I didn't allow her to get to know him. They already knew one another. Have you forgotten how often he used to come to the house?'

'But she was a kid.'

'She was when you and Mike broke up—'

'Like I said, a kid.'

'—but old enough to recognise him again when she saw him.' Maggie sighed. 'And she knew nothing about why you sacked him, and it wasn't something I'd discussed with her since. I never thought it might become a problem. He was out of our life—out of all our lives. Or so I thought.'

'But now he's back again?'

'Yes.'

'Doing what, exactly?'

Maggie lifted her shoulders. 'Your guess is as good as mine. All I know is that Lindsey is crazy about him, and she won't listen to any objections I make.'

Neil hesitated. 'Is he sleeping with her?'

Maggie's face flamed. It was ridiculous, really, but his question was so unexpected, and she had forgotten what it was like to be that outspoken with a man. 'Um—I haven't asked her,' she admitted at last, wishing she'd anticipated what he might say. 'I doubt if he's capable of sustaining any other kind of relationship, and Lindsey's not—not unaware of sex.'

Neil's expression revealed his frustration. 'You mean she isn't a virgin?'

'I don't think so.' Maggie wished she'd never started this. 'Whether I like it or not, girls of Lindsey's age are sexually active. They get the Pill as soon as they're old enough to be interested in boys. I might not have, but society has recognised that teenagers will experiment, and it's better that they're protected than not.'

Neil half turned in his seat towards her. 'Since when have you become so knowledgeable about what teenagers think?' he asked softly, and Maggie felt the draught of his warm breath against her cheek.

'Since I was obliged to cope as a single parent,' she responded stiffly, refusing to look at him. 'I'm sure you think it's all my fault, but, as I said earlier, Lindsey's too old to be told who she can and cannot date.'

Neil frowned. 'What did you say when she first told you she was going out with Reynolds?'

Maggie slumped back against the cushions. 'She didn't tell me. At least, not initially. I don't know if he'd told her to keep it quiet, but they'd been seeing one another for almost three months before I found out.'

'And how did you find out?'

'He told me.' Her lips twisted. 'He called at the shop one afternoon when I was alone, and took great pleasure in relaying the fact that he was Lindsey's new boyfriend. I knew she'd been seeing someone, but I'd assumed it was a boy she used to know. Mike said he'd been dating her since the night of the party, and that she was mad about him. And she was—*is*.'

Neil was silent for so long that she was obliged to look at him, half afraid of what she might see in his gaze. But to her surprise—and dismay—his eyes were fixed on her anxious face, and she froze into startled immobility when he reached out and brushed her cheek with the back of his hand.

'Poor Mags,' he said, drawing his fingers across her parted lips. 'I can imagine how you felt when he said that. He always admired you, you know, so perhaps Lindsey is just a substitute. Not to mention what he thought he had to gain from it.'

Maggie blinked. 'You're not angry?'

Neil shrugged. 'Sure I am, but I'm coming to terms with it. Besides, why should I give him the satisfaction? It would serve him right if I chose to call his bluff.'

'But you can't.' Maggie was horrified.

'Why can't I?'

'Well, because you can't want Lindsey to go out with a snake like him.'

'But as you said,' he pointed out softly, 'it's not as if she was totally innocent. And Reynolds will soon get sick when he finds his plan isn't working.'

Maggie stared at him. 'I don't believe this.'

'What don't you believe?'

'That—that you'd abandon your daughter to get back at me.'

'At you?' Neil was taken aback. 'What has it got to do with you?'

Maggie swallowed. 'That—that crack, about him admiring me; what did you mean by that?'

Neil's eyes widened. 'I didn't mean anything,' he said innocently. 'But Mike was attracted to you. You knew that.'

'Well, I wasn't attracted to him.' Maggie eyed him fiercely. 'You're not implying that I'm in league with him or anything?'

'In league with Mike Reynolds?' Neil's lips twisted. 'Now there's a novelty.'

'Because I'm not,' she added firmly. 'I can't think of anyone I dislike more.'

'Not even me?' he taunted her, trailing provocative fingers down her sleeve, and Maggie shivered in spite of herself.

'No. Not even you,' she assured him tightly, lifting her arm to remove his teasing caress. 'Don't play with me, Neil. I'm serious. There must be something we can do.'

'Oh, there is.'

Neil's words—and the sensual caress of his eyes—caused a blistering wave of heat to engulf her. Her hands, which had been cold, were now slippery with sweat, and she could feel the awareness that had started in the bath centred like a pulse low in her stomach.

'Wh-what?' she asked jerkily, looking anywhere but at him. God, did he know what he was doing to her, or was he just testing his famous charm?

'Ride with it,' he declared, startling her into another unwary appraisal. 'As I see it, Lindsey wouldn't want to be with him if he wasn't treating her well. I was mad, sure, when you first told me, but that's what he wants. Don't you see? He expects me to come rushing back to London. When I don't, he's going to be seriously disappointed.'

Maggie stared at him disbelievingly. 'But you said—'

'What did I say?'

'You said there was something we could do.'

'There is.' His arm was along the back of the seat behind her, and now she could feel his fingers toying with the ends of her silky blonde hair. 'We can spend a pleasant evening together. It'll be like old times. Before your ego—and Oliver Massey—got in the way.'

Maggie felt like bursting into tears. This couldn't be happening, she thought. Not only was Neil refusing to help her, but he seemed to think her coming here had given him some divine right to torment her, not just mentally but physically as well. When his fingers brushed her neck, she almost jumped a mile, and when Neil's hand descended on her shoulder, she thrust her empty glass onto the table and tried to move away.

'Mags,' he said, and even the way he said her name caused every nerve in her body to tingle, 'why shouldn't we enjoy this while it lasts?' He looped the veil of her hair behind her ear so that he could see her profile, his breath fanning her nape as he spoke. 'You know you want to. You're trembling so badly, you're in danger of shaking both of us off the sofa. Not that I'd object to that entirely. It wouldn't be the first time we'd made love on the floor.'

'M-made l-love?' she stammered, her eyes wide and panicky, gazing into his.

'Why not?' he asked, his free hand cupping her face, the pad of his thumb moving sensuously over the delicate contours of her ear. 'Don't tell me you've forgotten how good it always was between us.' His hand moved down, pausing so he could rub one swollen nipple with his palm, before coming to rest on her knee. 'You used to tell me you ached,' he added, his thumb defining the separation of her legs. 'Here,' he said, his voice uneven, but when he would have lifted the hem of her skirt she brought both hands down to stop him.

'No.'

'No?'

Patently, he didn't believe her, and she couldn't altogether blame him. Dear God, her muscles were shaking with the effort of holding her knees together, when all she really wanted to do was open her legs.

'We can't,' she insisted unsteadily, wishing his lean, dark face weren't so destructively sensual in the lamplight. His narrowed eyes were watching her mouth, and almost instinctively, it seemed, her tongue emerged to moisten her parted lips.

He disturbed her so much. He always had. She felt like someone who had been lost in the desert, desperate for water, and who had suddenly come upon a pool of fresh clean water. She was dying of thirst; she wanted to plunge in; but she was afraid it was a mirage—that if she took that final step she'd find it was only sand.

She tried to distract herself by dissecting his features. What was there about him that held her so in thrall? Hooded eyes, narrow cheekbones, a thin, almost cruel mouth should not hold such power over her. Yet she knew her control was as fragile as gossamer. If he touched her, her resistance would shatter like a mirror.

'Why can't we?' he countered, permitting her to prevent his hand from exploring farther, but not giving up. He bent towards her, the edges of his shirt parting to reveal the brown column of his throat, and caught her earlobe between his teeth. He bit her, hard enough to hurt, but not hard enough to do any real damage. 'I want to touch you, Maggie. Don't you want to touch me?'

Did she?

Maggie quivered. 'I am touching you,' she said, gripping his hand in her lap still tighter. 'But I think I ought to go to bed. I—I've got to be up early in the morning.'

'Well, I agree about going to bed,' murmured Neil, transferring his attention to the curve of her neck. She felt his tongue making sensuous circles against her flesh, and wondered how much more of this she could take without giving in. 'Mmm, you smell nice. I guess you're still using the same perfume. Do you still cover all your pulse-points like you used to? Well, most of them,' he amended, loosening the buttons at the neckline of the skinny-rib sweater. 'There are certain points I wouldn't want to contaminate with artificial scents.'

'Neil!'

'What?' His face was only inches from hers now, and she could see the raw sexuality in his gaze. That, and something else she didn't recognise, and which she was too distraught to worry about at that moment.

'Don't do this,' she wailed, but he had never obeyed her.

'Do what?' he breathed. 'Do this——?' He brushed her lips with his tongue. 'Or this——?' He cupped her nape and tipped her face up to his. 'Or do you mean this?' he asked, with sudden harshness, and his lips covered her protesting mouth.

Maggie's resistance snapped. Desire, hot and strong, swept through her veins, quickening her pulse and thickening her blood. She could hear it pounding in her head, could feel the hammering beat of her heart in her chest. The sound was thundering in her ears, deafening her to any voice of caution. It had been so long since Neil had held her in his arms, so long since she had felt anything but bitter regret.

Their mouths parted and came together, once, twice, and then clung, his tongue pushing its way between her teeth to take possession of her in the way no one else ever had. She'd wanted Neil since she'd first seen him watching her on the catwalk all those years ago. She'd been excited then, and she was excited now. She felt like a teenager again.

He pushed her back against the soft cushions behind her, kissing her hungrily—angrily?—almost hurting her in his need to ravish her mouth. One hand held her head still as he made a nonsense of her plea for restraint, while the other pushed up her skirt and caressed her thigh.

Even through her pantihose, he must be able to tell what he was doing to her, she thought painfully. The tips of his fingers were wet from her arousal, her legs splayed now as she had wanted to splay them before. If only she'd been wearing stockings, she thought, aching for him to slide inside her. But in the absence of that she wanted to touch him, and her hands groped eagerly for his zip.

And then she knew.

Her cheeks flamed even now, at the memory of it. God, what must he have been thinking of her? What perverted sense of pleasure had it given him to prove she was like putty in his hands? She had been so stupid, so gullible. So lacking in any moral fibre that he had only had to kiss her for her to fall apart.

While he...

Her throat constricted. She wished now that she had never attempted to unzip his trousers. Maybe if she hadn't some hint, some element in the way he was holding her would have warned her that his embrace was not what it seemed.

But she had reached for him. Her hands had fastened on the buckle of his belt at first, but then the desire to feel his hard arousal throbbing beneath the cloth had driven her hands lower. With impatience getting in the way of self control, she had stroked her fingers across his groin—and discovered he wasn't aroused at all.

She shivered, the horror she had felt then attacking her again. She remembered she'd drawn back as if his thigh had burned her fingers. And perhaps it had, though with acid, not with fire.

How could he? she thought, feeling the tears that had punctuated her sleep pricking her eyes again. He had been callous to her before, but never so deliberately cruel. It was as if he'd wanted to punish her, to prove to her that however she might regret the past he hadn't changed. He hadn't forgiven her for betraying him with Oliver Massey. She knew now that he never would.

She finished applying her make-up, doing her best to disguise the dark rings around her eyes that had been accentuated by the uneasy night she had just spent. It was late, already after nine; as often happened, she had fallen into a deep slumber just before dawn. Consequently, she had overslept, and she hoped Neil imagined she had done so because she had nothing on her conscience.

She sighed. Her whereabouts notwithstanding, the thought of staying in bed was still her favourite option. But not this bed, not Neil's bed, she thought, regarding the tumbled covers behind her without liking. Not that this was Neil's bed, except in the way that everything in this house belonged to him.

Except herself, she thought bitterly, and that was hardly a convincing admission. She would have been his, if he'd let her. If he'd wanted her, as she had wanted him. Until she'd discovered that, for all his pretence of passion, his emotions weren't even involved.

Somehow—she still wasn't precisely sure how—she'd got away from him, and found her way to her room. He hadn't made any attempt to detain her. As she'd scrambled to regain her dignity, as she'd pushed down her skirt and got to her feet, on legs that were decidedly shaky, Neil had lain back against the cushions, watching her with narrowed, mocking eyes. Enjoying her confusion, she thought frustratedly. Letting her make her exit, like the rejected slut he thought she was.

She dragged herself up from the stool and reached for her sweater. She wished now she'd worn something more glamorous, but she hadn't wanted him to think that she had done so to arouse his interest. Oh, God! The irony of that struck her again with painful magnitude. She'd been lying to herself when she'd come here. She'd still be lying to herself when she left.

Fortunately, her hair needed little attention. It was so straight, she used to joke when she was young that it actually turned the other way when she tried to curl it. However, becoming a model had taught her to make the most of her assets, and since she was fifteen she had relied on the way it was cut to give it style. These days, it was longer than it used to be, and she used a metal barrette to hold it back at one side.

When she was satisfied there was nothing more she could do to improve her appearance, she packed her belongings into her holdall, picked up her bag and left the room. Her coat was downstairs, where Mrs Fenwick had hung it the night before. She would ask the housekeeper to phone for a taxi. She had no desire to run into Neil again.

She had bargained without taking Luke's presence into consideration. As she came down the stairs, he came out of a room on the left of the hall. It wasn't the drawing room or the dining room, where they had had supper the previous evening. She guessed it might be Neil's study, but with tightening nerves she hoped it wasn't.

'Hey...' Luke was his usual cheery self, limping across the hall to greet her, and looking in some surprise at the bag she was carrying. 'What's going on?' he asked. 'You've not had breakfast, have you? Neil said he thought you must be tired, but I know he doesn't expect you to leave without having something to eat.'

'I'm not hungry, Luke.' Maggie looked about her with apprehension. She licked her dry lips. 'Where is he?'

'Oh, he won't be long,' Luke assured her, unwittingly misinterpreting her question. 'He and Nicola have gone to the stables. One of the mares has just had a foal and she wanted to see it.'

Maggie's stomach hollowed. 'Nicola?' Who the hell was Nicola?

'Yes. Nicola Braithwaite,' said Luke easily. 'Her father owns the land to the north of the estate. She's often about. You may remember her. She used to be called Nicola Armstrong. She got married around the time you and Neil were—well—splitting up.' He flushed. 'Her marriage didn't work out either. She got a divorce last year.'

'I see.'

Maggie blinked. Oh, yes, she thought tensely, she remembered Nicola Armstrong. When Neil had first bought the house on the Haversham estate, Nicola had been instrumental in introducing him to the neighbourhood. She had claimed to be one of his most ardent fans, but Maggie had thought Nicola admired him because he was famous. In any event her motives had not been one-sided. She had befriended Neil for her own purposes rather than his.

Not that Neil had ever shown any interest in her; not to Maggie's knowledge anyway. But that was five years ago.

Times had changed. Nicola's ambitions might finally be going to bear fruit.

'Come and have some coffee,' Luke urged now, attempting to steer her back the way he had come. 'Neil usually has breakfast in the morning room. It often gets the sun at this time of day. Not this morning, of course,' he added ruefully. 'I expect you've noticed there's been a covering of snow overnight.'

'No, I hadn't noticed,' murmured Maggie tightly, realising she had been too absorbed with her own worries to pay any attention to the weather. She knew a moment's panic. 'It hasn't blocked the roads or anything, has it? I mean—' she coloured now '—I wouldn't want anything to hold me up.'

Luke gave her a doubtful look. 'You are leaving, then?'

'Of course.' Maggie endeavoured to sound cheerful. 'You knew I was only staying overnight, didn't you?'

Luke drew a breath. 'I suppose so,' he said, leading the way into the room, where a morning newspaper, deposited carelessly on a chair, indicated where he had been having his breakfast. 'Sit down, won't you? I'll ask Mrs Fenwick to bring us some fresh coffee. Then you can tell me all about London—and Lindsey.'

'Oh, please…' Maggie just wanted to get away—without seeing Neil, if that was possible. 'Do you know the number of a local taxi firm? I want to hire a cab.'

Luke, who had been about to subside into his chair again, turned to stare at her. 'A cab?' he said, shaking his head. 'That won't be necessary, Maggie. If Neil's too busy to drive you into Newcastle, I'll take you. I told him last night: I'm not helpless. I can still drive a car.'

Maggie sighed. 'Oh, Luke—'

But what she had been about to say remained unspoken as a door slammed and voices sounded in the hall. Oh, God, Maggie thought as a woman laughed, it was Neil and Nicola. Had Neil told her she was here? She could imagine Nicola's contempt if Neil had told her what had happened last night.

Luke limped past her, with scarcely a glance in her direction. 'We're in here, Neil,' he called, proving once again that his allegiance was to the other man. 'Hello, Nicky,' she heard him continue, with his usual sociability. 'You look cold. There's a fire in the drawing room, if you'd like to go in there.'

'What I'd really like is some coffee,' declared Nicola firmly, and now Maggie was convinced the woman knew Neil's ex-wife was here. She wanted to make sure Maggie saw them together. She wasn't about to lose a chance to gloat.

'Oh.'

To his credit, Luke sounded slightly taken aback, and Maggie wondered if she'd misjudged his motives. Perhaps he had been hoping to divert Nicola into the drawing room, if only to give Neil an opportunity to speak to Maggie privately.

It was obvious they were all coming into the morning room, and Maggie stood, gripping the back of one of the dining chairs with white-knuckled fingers. It didn't help that she was prepared for their appearance, or that the leaden sky filtered the light coming into the room and disguised the shadows on her cheeks. She still felt like an intruder, a situation which she was sure Nicola would enjoy exploiting to the full.

CHAPTER FIVE

SHE should have sat down.

Maggie realised that as soon as they appeared in the doorway. As it was, she looked as if she was afraid to relax in Neil's house, as if she was afraid of him.

'Maggie!' As she'd half expected, it was Nicola who took the initiative, coming round the table to greet her, as if she, and not Maggie, had once been the mistress here. 'Neil said you'd come to see him. How are you? And how's that pretty daughter of yours? She must be—oh, nearly twenty by now.'

'She's seventeen,' said Maggie stiffly, noticing it was her hand, and not Nicola's, that was as cold as ice. She exchanged a guarded look with her ex-husband. 'Neil's her father. Haven't you asked him?'

Nicola released Maggie's hand, and glanced over her shoulder. 'Oh, Neil and I talk about all sorts of things,' she said, implying an intimacy that Maggie was quite prepared to believe. She moved away and pressed the bell that summoned Mrs Fenwick. 'Do you want coffee, darling? I'm absolutely dying for some caffeine myself.'

Darling?

Maggie's legs felt decidedly unsteady, and, pulling the chair away from the table, she felt her way round it, lowering herself onto its gold buttoned seat like an old woman. Dear God, were they engaged? Was that what Nicola was trying oh, so indiscreetly to tell her? Why hadn't Neil told her himself? She couldn't believe it was because he hadn't wanted to hurt her feelings.

'Sure. Why not?' he remarked now, in answer to Nicola's question, but instead of sitting at the table he went to stand beside the window, staring out at the lowering clouds without expression.

He was wearing a tweed jacket this morning, over a cream knitted shirt and narrow cords. His outfit almost exactly matched that of the other woman, except that she was wearing jodhpurs and knee-length boots. In addition to which, a loose scarf was knotted about Nicola's shoulders, the ends trailing elegantly across her sleeve. It was green Paisley, and drew attention to the russet strands of her hair, which she wore in a netted chignon at her nape.

'Neil said you arrived last evening,' Nicola prompted now, and Maggie wondered if she intended to ask her why she'd come. Maybe, if she was engaged to Neil, she considered she had that right. After all, she could be mistress here before too long.

'Did you ring, Mr Jordan?'

Mrs Fenwick's polite enquiry was to her employer, and Maggie saw her lips tighten a little when Nicola chose to reply. 'I did, Mrs Fenwick,' she said tersely. 'Can we have some fresh coffee, please? Oh—and you can clear these dirty dishes. I think Mr Parry has finished, haven't you, Luke?'

Luke seemed to have lost his appetite, and he pushed his plate towards Mrs Fenwick with a rueful grin. 'Sorry about that, Mrs Fenwick,' he said. 'I guess I wasn't as hungry as I thought. No more coffee for me. I've had enough.'

'How about you, madam?' asked the housekeeper, addressing herself to Maggie. 'Would you like something to eat? I couldn't help noticing that you didn't eat much at supper, and it's a cold day to go without something warm inside you.'

Nicola's lips thinned. 'Why, yes, Maggie,' she said, as if that had been her intention all along. 'If I were you I'd have a good meal before you go.' Her smile was malicious, but only Maggie was aware of it. 'I'm sure you enjoy your food. Just tell Mrs Fenwick what you'd like.'

It was all Maggie could do not to tell her to mind her own business. Her smug remark made Maggie's blood boil. Still, at least she'd never been as thin as a beanpole, even when she was modelling. There wasn't an ounce of spare flesh on Nicola's bony frame.

'I think Maggie can decide for herself, don't you?' remarked Neil suddenly, as if sensing that the situation was in danger of exploding. He didn't turn, but Maggie guessed he was aware of her resentment. Perhaps he was afraid she'd tell his girlfriend what had happened the night before. However badly it had turned out, it would be hard to explain why he'd come on to her as he had.

'Well, of course.'

But Nicola didn't like him reproving her, and Maggie enjoyed the brief sense of victory while she could. 'Really, Mrs Fenwick,' she said, conscious that Nicola was listening to every word, 'coffee would be fine.' She smiled. 'But thank you for asking. I must say, if I lived here for long, I'd have to watch my weight, too.'

Neil turned, his hands thrust somewhat aggressively into his jacket pockets. 'Thank you, Mrs Fenwick,' he said, dismissing the housekeeper with an ease Maggie could only admire. Then he came to stand behind the chair opposite her, regarding her with an enigmatic gaze.

The table was round, a concession to the room's intimacy, she supposed, for, although it was still larger than any of the rooms in her town house, compared to the impressive drawing room, and the dining room where they had had supper the night before, this was a much more modest apartment. Maggie felt comfortable in it, but that didn't stop her from feeling apprehensive when he addressed himself to her.

'Did you sleep well?'

It was not what she had expected, and for a moment Maggie could only stare at him with wide, uncomprehending eyes. Not what Nicola—or Luke—had expected either, she guessed. What *had* they expected him to do? Admonish her for playing Nicola at her own game?

'Um—reasonably,' she muttered at last, finding she couldn't tell an outright lie and say she'd had a good night. 'I—I was just asking Luke if he'd call me a taxi. There's a train from Newcastle at about twelve-thirty, and I'd like to catch it.'

'And I've said there's no need for her to call a cab,' declared Luke, having taken the weight off his leg and resumed his seat. 'Really, Neil, I can take her to catch her train. I've got to collect that feed from Hexham anyway.'

'I'll take her myself,' said Neil, as if that settled the matter, and Maggie felt like some unwanted parcel they were passing around.

'I'm getting a cab,' she said, her expression brooking no argument. 'Now, does anyone know the number of the local taxi company, or do I have to ask Mrs Fenwick to look it up?'

It was late afternoon when Maggie let herself into her house in Prince's Crescent. Situated in a pleasant oasis just off Knightsbridge, the house was the first property she had owned outright, and she was proud as well as very fond of it. When she and Neil had split up, it had been important for her to have a place of her own that was every bit as fashionable as the house they had shared in Buckinghamshire. It had salved her pride somewhat to know that 24 Prince's Crescent had cost him an arm and a leg. It had given her a central base to work from, too, as she was to be concentrating all her energies on building up her own business from then on.

The house was tall and narrow, and she had to mount several steps to her front door. A second set of area steps led down to the basement, which she'd furnished independently from the house, and rented to the young man who looked after her books.

It had been convenient, too, having a man on the premises, so to speak. Herself and Lindsey, living alone, had seemed far too attractive a target. In consequence, Ray looked after the house while she was away, and was always there for protection, if she needed him.

Despite the cold air outside, the house felt pleasantly warm as she stepped into the hall. Home at last, she thought gratefully, closing the door and leaning back against it. The way she felt right now, she never wanted to leave it again.

The answering machine was blinking, and, relieved that

Lindsey hadn't erased her messages in her absence, Maggie took off her coat and draped it over the banister while the tape rewound.

There were perhaps half a dozen calls, mostly from friends or acquaintances, inviting her to either a party or a reception they were giving. Maggie didn't go out a lot, but in her line of work she met an awful lot of people who did. Most of whom liked parties, she acknowledged ruefully. How long was it since she had given a party? Far too long.

The only call she ought to return was from her sister.

Jacqueline—or Jackie, as she was usually called—had rung to find out if she was back. 'Give me a ring when you get in,' she'd added, with evident enthusiasm. 'I'm dying to know what happened. I hope you told that selfish bastard that he's to blame for Lindsey's being the way she is. She certainly doesn't get her arrogant ego from us.'

Maggie switched off the machine and stood for a moment with her hand pressed to her chest. The idea of ringing Jackie had no appeal whatsoever, and she decided to put it off until later. She wasn't looking forward to having to tell her sister that she had had no luck in persuading Neil to get involved. Apart from which, the whole subject was still too painful, and tomorrow might be time enough to relay the news.

Not that she had any intention of telling Jackie everything. There were some things that were just too personal to discuss. Jackie would understand when she told her she'd been disappointed. And weary, she thought, with a pang. She felt like nothing so much as crawling into bed.

The thought of bed, and its attendant quietness, reminded her that the house was unusually silent. No one had come to greet her on her arrival, and nor had any of the lights been lit. But, conversely, nor had the alarm been activated. Her daily woman would be long gone, but she knew Mrs Lewis would have set the alarm before she left.

Which meant Lindsey must have come home from school and gone out again, without giving a thought to security. It was typical of her indifference to her mother's requests, but right now Maggie was more concerned with where she was. Lindsey was supposed to have spent last night at Jackie's, but her sister hadn't mentioned whether she had.

Leaving her coat where it was, Maggie climbed the stairs to the first floor sitting room. Because the house was narrow, the ground floor was given over to her study, another bathroom, and the domestic offices. In consequence, the living and dining areas were on the first floor, with the bedrooms and their adjoining bathrooms on the floor above.

Maggie was tired, both in mind and body, but she knew she couldn't settle in for the evening until she knew where Lindsey was. She would have a shower, and a change of clothes, and then she'd make some phone calls, she decided. With a bit of luck, Lindsey would be at her friend's house. Perhaps she'd call Heather's mother before she did anything else.

She was going into the sitting room to use the phone when she heard a sound from upstairs. Immediately, every nerve in her body went on full alert, and the knowledge that without the alarm an intruder could have got into the house turned her mouth as dry as parchment. Notwithstanding the urge to escape down the stairs and out into the street, she moved to the foot of the second staircase and looked up into the darkness. 'Is anyone there?' she called foolishly, not knowing what she would do if it was an intruder, and then almost collapsed on the spot when a light was switched on and her daughter appeared at the head of the stairs.

'*Lindsey!*'

For a moment, Maggie could only stare at her daughter in weak disbelief, but then the anxiety she had felt as she'd climbed the stairs reasserted itself. Judging by her face, the girl had no conception of the shock she had given her mother, and Maggie's tone was sharper than it might have been as she gazed up at the sulky teenager.

'What on earth are you doing?' she demanded. 'Scaring me like that! Do you want me to have a heart attack or something?'

'I didn't hear you come in,' said Lindsey sullenly. 'Aunt Jackie said you wouldn't be back till later. What are you doing here anyway? I thought you'd go straight to the shop.'

'Well, as you can see, I didn't.' Maggie's brows drew together as she noticed, for the first time, what Lindsey was wearing. 'You're not ill, are you?' she asked, indicating the satin dressing gown Neil had sent the girl for Christmas. 'You have been to school, haven't you? I'll soon find out if you haven't.'

'Yes, I've been to school,' responded Lindsey aggressively. 'I—I was just getting changed.' She paused. 'Are you going out again?'

Maggie's nostrils flared. 'Why?' After the day she had had, her daughter's attitude was the last straw.

'Because I was going to ask Heather over!' exclaimed Lindsey defensively. 'And as I don't have a sitting room of my own I thought we might play some CDs on the stereo. It's not often I have the place to myself.'

Which was true. Maggie acknowledged that. Her own nocturnal habits meant that Lindsey was not often alone in the house. She never tired of reminding her mother that when they'd lived in Buckinghamshire she had had a whole suite of rooms to herself. But that didn't mean she was keen to go and stay with her father these days. For all she might crave more luxurious surroundings, without anyone to impress, it was no fun.

'Well, I'm sorry,' said Maggie now, feeling the burden of responsibility bearing down on her. 'I'm just too tired to move another step.' She squared her shoulders. 'Anyway, you haven't asked me about your father. Aren't you interested to know why I went?'

'I am.'

Maggie sucked in her breath. It wasn't her daughter who had spoken, but the man who had stepped into view behind her. Mike Reynolds, wearing Lindsey's old towelling bathrobe, now looked down at her with mocking eyes. And, although Lindsey looked slightly taken aback, clearly he felt he had nothing to hide. 'Hi, Maggie.'

Maggie didn't have to ask what he was doing here. She now understood Lindsey's reasons for not noticing her return, and why she was wrapped in the satin robe and noth-

ing else. She wanted to scream and rage, and order the
gloating bastard out of her house. But experience had made
her wary, and instead she turned her back on both of them
and strode into the sitting room.

The lamplit room soothed her raw nerves. Although these
days she seldom took a drink, she reached for the decanter
of whisky, and poured herself a small measure. Then, cra-
dling the glass between her palms, she wandered restlessly
over to the windows. Staring out at the shadowy Crescent
below, she wondered what on earth she was going to do
now.

The sound of someone coming down the stairs made her
stiffen, and when Mike Reynolds sauntered into the room
she knew she had been right to feel apprehensive. She could
see his face, mirrored in the darkened window, and there
was such a look of satisfaction on it that she wished she
owned some kind of weapon. She could think of nothing
more appealing than knocking that smug expression off his
face.

'Hey, I could do with one of those,' he said as she turned
to face him, indicating the glass in her hand. 'How about
being sociable and making me one? This seems like as
good a time as any to talk.'

Maggie didn't move. 'Where's Lindsey?'

'Oh, don't worry about Lin,' he said carelessly. 'She's
taking a shower. We got kind of hot and sweaty—if you
can remember how that feels.'

Maggie wouldn't let him provoke her. Taking a sip of
her drink, she managed to keep her hand from shaking.
'You're wasting your time,' she said. 'Neil's not going to
do what you wanted. As far as he's concerned you can have
her. He doesn't care what you do, so long as you leave him
alone.'

Mike's eyes narrowed. 'You'd better be joking.'

'Do I look like I'm joking?' Maggie was amazed at how
casual she appeared. 'No, I'm not joking, Mike. He's
changed. He doesn't need us any more. And your little
threats are not going to achieve anything.'

Mike stared at her uncertainly. 'I don't believe you.'

'No?' Maggie shrugged. 'Well, I don't care what you

believe, Mike. As far as I'm concerned, it was a wasted journey. And not one I'd like to repeat,' she added, more for her benefit than his.

Mike scowled, and, evidently deciding she wasn't about to offer him any hospitality, he went to help himself to a drink. He poured a generous measure of Scotch, threw it to the back of his throat, and then poured himself another. And, although Maggie had no sympathy for him, she couldn't help thinking she knew exactly how he felt.

'Jerk! Bastard!'

The epithets came thick and fast, and Maggie had to turn away for fear he might see the tremulous hope that flared inside her. Could Neil have been right? Could the fact that he was apparently indifferent to whoever his daughter went out with work in their favour? She hadn't believed it at the time, but suddenly it didn't seem so incredible after all.

'He won't get away with it.'

Mike's next words brought her round again, and although she was trying hard not to feel smug she couldn't hide the exhilaration in her voice. 'Why not?' she asked. 'What can you possibly do that you haven't already done?'

'I don't know.' Mike looked down at the liquid in his glass, before once more swallowing it in one gulp. 'But I'll think of something,' he said, depositing the glass on a polished table. 'Tell Lindsey I'll ring her,' he added, striding towards the door.

Maggie waited until she heard the front door slam behind him before moving to lift the glass before it could stain the wood. Already, a film of dampness had formed beneath it, and she used a paper napkin from the tray to dry it off.

But the minor inconvenience of removing a patch of dampness was nothing. Inside her, the feeling of exhilaration was spreading, and she could hardly keep a smile off her face. Whatever he said, she couldn't believe Mike had wanted her daughter for anything more than what he thought he could get out of the relationship. That was why he'd waited three months before telling her about it. He'd wanted to be sure Lindsey was well and truly hooked before he showed his hand.

And now what could he do? she asked herself tremulously. He'd done his worst, and it hadn't gained him anything. She shook her head. She would have to write to Neil and apologise. Or at least tell him that his cunning plan had worked.

'Where's Mike?'

She had been so wrapped up in her own excitement that she hadn't heard her daughter come downstairs. Lindsey stood in the doorway now, a slim wraith of a girl in black leggings and a thigh-length sweater, the cuffs almost covering her hands as she supported herself against the door. Her long dark hair—hair that so much resembled Neil's, Maggie realised with a sudden pang—was loose about her shoulders. Her feet were bare, the nails painted scarlet, to match the slash of colour on her mouth.

Maggie swallowed. 'He's gone.'

'Gone?' Lindsey stared at her accusingly. 'Why has he gone? What did you say to him?'

'Don't you take that tone with me, young woman.' Maggie could feel the brief surge of energy she had experienced when Mike had departed dispersing in the face of her daughter's anger. 'He has no right to be in this house, let alone—let alone anything else.' She squared her shoulders. 'Are you sure you've been to school today? Did you spend last night at Aunt Jackie's?'

Lindsey's mouth turned down. 'Yes,' she said, with exaggerated patience. 'Mike was in Holland until today; you know that. And why shouldn't I invite him here? This is my home as well as yours.'

'Your home—but not your love-nest!' declared Maggie coldly. 'You knew you'd done wrong; that's why you were hoping I was going out again. It wasn't your idea for him to show himself.' Her anxiety surfaced. 'Can't you see how he's using you, you silly little—?'

Lindsey stiffened. 'You don't understand,' she said passionately. 'Just because your relationships turn bad is no reason to criticise mine. Mike loves me; he's told me. And I love him. And before you tell me he's too old for me again I want you to know I prefer an older man.'

Maggie shook her head. 'You don't understand...'

'What don't I understand?'

Maggie hesitated. 'You don't know why I went to see your father, for a start.'

'Yes, I do.' Lindsey was contemptuous. 'Oh, you thought Mike hadn't told me. Well, yes, he did, as it happens. He said you were going to ask him to make another album.'

Maggie was stunned. And then, recovering, she asked, 'Did he tell you why?'

'Yes.' Lindsey tossed her head. 'He's in financial difficulties, and he says Dad owes him.' She turned away. 'If it wasn't for him, Dad wouldn't be where he is today.'

CHAPTER SIX

'SO YOU think Neil might be going to get married again?'

'I didn't say that.' Maggie moved the half-eaten piece of chicken round her plate. 'I just said he and Nicola appear to be very close. But I doubt if either of them is in any hurry to hear wedding bells. They've both got broken marriages behind them, remember?'

'All the same...'

Jackie was obviously loath to let it go, and Maggie wished she had cried off their weekly lunch at Luigi's. Ever since she'd got back from Northumberland, her sister had been pressing her for information about her trip, and although Maggie had told her that Neil had refused to do anything about his daughter's relationship with Mike Reynolds her sister seemed more interested in the interaction between herself and her ex-husband than anything else.

Which wasn't so surprising, really, considering Jackie still resented Neil for the way he had treated her sister. Maggie suspected her greatest fear was that she and Neil might have found some common ground in their concern for their daughter, and her continuing demand for details was to reassure herself that nothing untoward had happened.

Maggie's lips twisted as she looked round the exclusive little restaurant. If only Jackie knew, she thought, feeling the heat rising beneath her skin at the memory of how she had behaved. Her sister had been right to worry, had she but known it. Though not about Neil, Maggie reflected bitterly. His only remaining desire was to humiliate her.

'Imagine him buying that big old house,' Jackie continued, undaunted by her sister's obvious unwillingness to talk. 'Still, if he's thinking of getting married again, perhaps he'll have some more children. I know when Lindsey was born he was disappointed because she wasn't a boy.'

'That's not true!' Maggie couldn't allow Jackie to get away with something so outrageous. 'You know as well as I do that Neil positively doted on Lindsey when she was a baby.'

'Well, that's not what I thought,' retorted Jackie, sipping from her glass of wine. 'Neil's a chauvinist; admit it. Good heavens, Maggie, that's why you got a divorce.'

It wasn't, but Maggie had no intention of going into that. Instead, she placed her knife and fork on her plate, and looked round for the waiter. She had hardly touched her food, but that wasn't anything new. Since she'd returned from Northumberland four days ago, her appetite had been practically non-existent.

'Are you in a hurry?'

Jackie was looking at her a little resentfully now, and Maggie struggled to maintain a calm façde. 'Not particularly,' she said. 'I've finished, that's all.' She looked at Jackie's almost empty plate. 'Did you want something else?'

'Well, I did think we might have a portion of Luigi's cheesecake,' Jackie declared, wiping her mouth on her napkin. Four years older than Maggie, and happily spreading into middle age, Jackie seldom bothered about her figure. If she wasn't exactly slim, she wasn't exactly fat either, and the customers in their south-coast shop preferred dealing with someone who wasn't thin as a rail.

Maggie forced herself to have patience. 'All right,' she said, even though the thought of the rich dessert made her feel slightly sick. Still, she consoled herself, she didn't have to eat it. And she was already aware of a certain tension between herself and her sister, because of her unwillingness to discuss her trip, that wouldn't be helped if she refused.

The waiter was summoned, and a few minutes later Jackie wiped the last smear of cream cheese from her lips. 'Oh, Maggie,' she said, 'that is truly ambrosia.' Then she frowned. 'Is something wrong with yours? Don't tell me seeing Neil has made you self-conscious about your weight again.'

'Of course not.' Maggie managed not to snap. But Jackie's constant carping about her ex-husband was wearing, particularly as it was unlikely that they would ever see him again. 'I guess I'm not hungry,' she added, refusing to be provoked. 'Do you want coffee?'

'Only if you're having some.'

Maggie's smile was tight. 'Why not?' she asked, once again lifting her hand to the waiter. But it irritated her that she was so edgy when Jackie was really only showing a sisterly concern. For heaven's sake, it was all over now. Lindsey hadn't seen Mike since he'd stormed out of the house.

Apparently deciding to abandon the subject of Maggie's trip, Jackie mentioned the fact that she had found a new assistant for the Bournemouth shop. She had been interviewing applicants yesterday, she said. And then asked, 'Did you know Lindsey had applied?'

Maggie's momentary relief vanished. 'Lindsey?' She felt totally amazed. 'But she's still at school. You know that.'

'I know that, and you know that, but it doesn't seem very high on Lindsey's list of priorities,' responded Jackie, carelessly. 'In any event, I didn't appoint her. She's got no experience, apart from anything else.'

Maggie was stunned. 'But how did she find out about it?'

'Does it matter?' Jackie shrugged. 'I may have mentioned it when she stayed over, or perhaps she heard you talking about it on the phone. It's not as if it was a deep dark secret, like your trip to Northumberland. Lindsey and I don't worry about things like that.'

Maggie took a breath. 'My trip to Northumberland was not a deep dark secret,' she declared, keeping her temper with difficulty. 'And Lindsey and I didn't use to have secrets before Mike Reynolds appeared on the scene.' She licked her lips. 'Are you saying she actually turned up for an interview?'

'Heavens, no.' Jackie appeared to be enjoying having her at a disadvantage, and she was in no hurry to satisfy

Maggie's concern. 'She rang—let me see...was it Tuesday or Wednesday?' She frowned. 'Yes, it was Wednesday. I asked her why she wanted a job, and she said it was to earn some money.'

'Lindsey's not short of money.'

'Mike Reynolds is,' remarked Jackie pleasantly, looking at her over the rim of her cup. 'I doubt even you'd be prepared to advance him a small loan, would you? And Lindsey wants to do her part to help him out.'

Maggie swallowed. 'But Lindsey—' She paused, realising how ridiculous this was going to sound, and then went on reluctantly, 'She's not seeing Mike at present.'

'Who says?' Jackie looked incredulous.

'Well—' Maggie hesitated. 'I suppose I do. She hasn't been out at all this week. She's come home straight from school and spent the evenings doing her homework.'

'Is that your assessment, or hers?'

Maggie pressed her lips together. 'She hasn't been out,' she insisted firmly.

'There are phones,' pointed out Jackie drily, 'and it's possible he's been away. He does still handle other entertainers, doesn't he? Perhaps he's trying to find other talent. If Neil's not going to play ball, he has to do something to pay his debts.'

Maggie felt really sick now. 'But why is he doing this?' she protested. 'He knows Neil's not going to help him. Why can't he leave Lindsey alone?'

'Perhaps he really cares for her,' observed Jackie, playing devil's advocate. 'Rather more than her selfish father, if I'm any judge.'

Maggie left her office early that evening.

Since trade had fallen off, she spent less and less time at the shops themselves, and more and more time at the office. It was becoming increasingly difficult to juggle their finances, and she wished now that she hadn't given in to Jackie's suggestion to expand. But the divorce—and her subsequent need to keep herself busy—had given her more time to think than she had liked. Besides, she had wanted

the shops to succeed, not just for herself but for Jackie and
Lindsey as well.

And Jackie had played a large part in her decision to
open the first shop, as she had reminded Neil when she was
in Northumberland. At the time, Jackie herself had been
going through an acrimonious divorce, and Maggie's idea
that they should consider opening a shop had been gratefully received. The choice of shop hadn't been in question,
with Maggie's knowledge of the fashion industry. And, although she had expressed doubts, Jackie had insisted that,
with her contacts, it was a natural progression.

But there were times, as now, when Maggie wondered
if she would have gone through with it if it hadn't been for
her sister. For all she had believed she wanted her independence, she had never seen herself as a businesswoman.
And, despite the rows she and Neil had had, she had never
ruled out the idea of having another child. Like many
events in her life, things had happened almost without her
volition. Not least, her brief involvement with Oliver
Massey, which had had such a devastating effect on the
marriage.

There were lights on in the first-floor sitting room, she
saw, when she found a parking space for her small car just
a few yards down from her house. Parking was not usually
a problem in the Crescent, but today there was a rain-
spattered Mercedes parked at her door. It would have been
easier, she reflected, if the houses had been given their own
garage, but although the properties in the Crescent were
elegant and well sought after they'd been built before the
motor car had become such an essential tool.

In consequence, she was wet by the time she had locked
the car and walked the dozen paces to her door. It had
started raining at lunchtime, just as she and Jackie were
leaving the restaurant, and now it was a steady downpour,
soaking everything in sight.

She had her key ready to insert in the lock when the
front door opened. Mrs Lewis stood aside for her to come
in, and Maggie was grateful for her consideration. But her
gratitude was cut short when the daily woman adopted a

conspiratorial air and, thrusting her face close to her employer's, whispered, 'You've got a visitor, Mrs Freeman.'

Mike!

Maggie put down her briefcase and removed her damp scarf, too annoyed at the thought that Mike Reynolds was here to correct Mrs Lewis's pronouncement. Maggie had always used her professional name in conjunction with the boutiques, and after she and Neil divorced she had decided to use it in her private life too. Unfortunately, Mrs Lewis was one of those women to whom the fact that Maggie had a daughter gave her a certain status. In consequence, she insisted on calling her *Mrs* Freeman, no matter how many times Maggie pointed out her mistake.

'Where's Lindsey?' Maggie asked now, wishing she wouldn't let the man's reappearance rattle her. If this was to be an attempt to tap her for money, she wanted her daughter to know about it. There were to be no more secrets, as far as she was concerned.

'She's not back yet,' replied Mrs Lewis, apparently disappointed by Maggie's reaction to her news. 'Mr Jordan wanted to see her, too, but I told him I didn't know when she'd be home.'

'Mr Jordan!'

Maggie hadn't yet recovered from the shock of thinking Mike Reynolds was waiting to see her, and despite her efforts to remain calm the idea that Neil was here, in her house, was enough to send her running up the stairs. But he wasn't here to see her, she reminded herself. Mrs Lewis had said he wanted to see Lindsey. If he was waiting, it was for their daughter's sake, not for hers.

'I stayed a bit later than normal to make him some tea,' called Mrs Lewis after her. 'I hope that's all right. He said he'd driven all the way from Newcastle. I expect you noticed his car outside.'

The Mercedes! Maggie nodded, and, realising she couldn't delay any longer, she continued on her way. 'Um—bring me a fresh pot, would you, Mrs Lewis?' she asked, gripping the banister. 'I could do with a cup of tea myself.'

By the time she reached the top of the stairs, Neil was

standing in the doorway to the sitting room. 'Hello, Maggie,' he said. 'I hope you don't mind. I insisted on waiting until Lindsey got home.'

Maggie managed a shrug, trying not to notice that he stepped aside abruptly when she approached him. It was as if he thought he might be corrupted if he so much as touched her, and instead of waiting for the tea Maggie went to pour herself something stronger.

'You might have a long wait,' she said, turning with the glass in her hand. It crossed her mind that this was hardly the image she wanted him to retain of her, but as he thought the worst of her anyway, did it really matter?

Neil stood across the room from her, dark and somehow brooding in his black leather jerkin and matching jeans. The last time he'd been here was to tell her he wasn't going to oppose her bid for Lindsey's custody. But that was five years ago now, and they'd both changed a lot since then.

'She's at school, isn't she?' he asked at last, and Maggie moved her shoulders in a dismissing gesture.

'Your guess is as good as mine,' she said, determining not to make it easy for him. He hadn't made it easy for her, and it crossed her mind to wonder if he'd brought Nicola along for the ride.

'What's that supposed to mean?' Neil's eyes narrowed. 'Is she cutting her classes?'

'As to that, you'd have to ask her tutor. But I have it on good authority that she's looking for a job.'

'A job?'

It amused Maggie to see his look of consternation. Although she'd told him what was going on with Lindsey, she had the feeling now that he hadn't truly believed her before. So what had he thought? she wondered. That she'd gone to see him for some unspoken reason of her own? Perhaps he thought he'd discovered the truth when he'd kissed her. That she'd had some crazy notion to lure him back.

'It's true.' Maggie put her glass aside now, without even touching the whisky. 'There was a job going at the Bournemouth shop, and she applied for it.'

Neil's dark eyebrows rose. 'At whose instigation?'

'Well, not mine,' said Maggie shortly, detecting the reproof. 'Jackie thinks it's her way of trying to help Mike Reynolds out of his difficulties. If he's short of money, that's presumably why he tried to blackmail you.'

Neil scowled. 'I hope you told him I didn't buy his offer?'

'Oh, yes.' Maggie crossed her arms across her midriff. 'He was here with Lindsey when I got back.'

'Here?'

'As in Lindsey's bedroom,' agreed Maggie crisply. 'I did warn you what he was like. He doesn't give up.'

Neil thrust his hands into his trouser pockets and stared down at the carpet. He didn't say anything, but Maggie noticed that the skin behind his ears was pink, which was a sure sign that he was mad. His lean face was drawn, too, and pale beneath his tan.

'I've brought you some sandwiches, Mrs Freeman.' Mrs Lewis bustled into the room at that moment, apparently unaware or indifferent to the fact that she hadn't knocked. 'I thought Mr Jordan might be hungry,' she added pleasantly, but Maggie wondered if curiosity was a stronger motivation. 'Will he be joining you for supper? I can put another casserole in the oven.'

'No, thank you.' Before Neil could refuse the invitation for himself, Maggie dived in. 'Are you leaving now, Mrs Lewis?' she continued pointedly. 'I'll see you on Monday, as usual.'

'Very well, Mrs Freeman.' This time, Maggie was sure the woman used the wrong title deliberately. 'Oh—I nearly forgot; that man, Mr Reynolds, phoned earlier. He asked me to tell Lindsey that he'll be out of town for a few days, but as I won't be here when she gets in perhaps you'd deliver the message. He says he'll be in touch with her as soon as he gets back.'

'Thank you, Mrs Lewis.'

Maggie didn't dare look at Neil as the housekeeper made her exit. She was half afraid he might accuse Mrs Lewis of being in league with Mike Reynolds, when in all honesty she was only doing her job. Nevertheless, at some point in the future she was going to have to ask the woman not to relay messages to Lindsey without informing her. If Mike Reynolds phoned, she wanted to know about it first.

When the door had closed again, and Mrs Lewis was heard descending the stairs, Neil looked up, his eyes dark with anger. 'Does this mean Lindsey will be coming home soon?' he enquired in a soft, menacing tone. 'For God's sake, why don't you change your phone number? Anything to stop that louse from reaching her.'

'And do you really think that would?' Maggie asked harshly. 'Grow up, Neil. He comes here. How am I supposed to keep him away?'

'You could forbid Lindsey to see him; ground her, or something. Stop her allowance.'

'I've done all those things,' said Maggie wearily. 'Why do you think I came to see you? I told you what was happening, but you were too busy making fun of me to take it seriously.'

Neil stared at her a moment more, and then flung himself onto the couch. 'I did take it seriously,' he muttered. 'Why the hell do you think I'm here? OK—so maybe things got out of hand, but you can't blame me for that. I didn't know you were starved for sex, did I? It was only a bit of fun, until you lost control.'

'*I* lost control!'

'Well, didn't you?' He was devastatingly direct. 'One minute we were talking about Lindsey, and the next you were practically throwing yourself at me. You can't blame me if I didn't react the way you expected.'

Maggie was trembling with anger. 'You swine!' She gripped the back of the sofa, staring down at him with vengeful eyes. 'It wasn't like that, Neil, and you know it. You deliberately forced the pace so that I'd give in.'

'Whatever...'

'Whatever, nothing!' She took a steadying breath. 'You're a cruel bastard, Neil, so why should I expect Lindsey to consider my feelings? Not when she's got your example to follow.'

Neil gave a weary sigh. 'Forget it, for God's sake. I have. And don't go blaming Lindsey for my faults. She's your

daughter just as much as mine; you raised her. If she's
rebelling now, perhaps you should ask yourself why.'

'Is that all you think this is? A teenage rebellion?' Maggie gave a mirthless laugh. 'Do you think if you wait long
enough it will go away? My God, she's in danger of ruining
her life, Neil, and you talk about rebellion! Lindsey's beautiful, she's bright, and intelligent, and she's fun to be with.
Mike Reynolds may have used her to get at you, but I don't
think he has any intention of letting her go.'

Neil's expression darkened. 'You're exaggerating.'

'Am I?' Maggie took a deep breath, and then, spreading
her hands, she moved away from the sofa. 'Perhaps I am.
Perhaps my own dislike of Mike is colouring my judgement. But this week I thought she hadn't seen him, and
now it turns out that they've been in touch all along.'

'So what do you want me to do?'

Maggie gave him a startled look. 'What do *I* want you
to do?'

'That's what I said.'

Maggie's brows drew together. 'I don't understand.
When I left Haversham, I understood you were quite happy
to let Lindsey go her own way. What's happened to make
you change your mind?' She caught her breath. 'Oh—he
hasn't been in touch with you himself?'

'No.' Neil lifted his shoulders, not looking at her. He
paused. 'Perhaps I'm not as stoical about their relationship
as I appeared.'

Maggie blinked. 'You mean—you're prepared to do as
he asked: come back to London and record another album?'
She shook her head. 'Oh, Neil, I don't know what to say.'

'Don't say anything,' he advised drily. 'I'm not committing myself one way or the other. First of all, I intend
to talk to Lindsey. To see if I can get through to her. I'll
let you know what I decide after that.'

Maggie moistened her lips. 'You're staying, then?'

Neil looked up at her wryly. 'Isn't that what you want?'

'No, I—' Maggie wrapped her arms about herself as if
she needed the protection. 'I mean—did you come alone?
Where are you staying?'

'Well, Luke didn't come with me, if that's what you

mean,' said Neil flatly. 'Apart from the fact that his leg's still troubling him, I prefer one of us to be around to handle any problems on the estate. But, in any case, I didn't invite him. This is between you and me, Maggie. And Lindsey, of course.'

Maggie didn't have the nerve to ask if Nicola had been invited. Just because she hadn't accompanied him to the house, that was no reason to assume she wasn't waiting at the hotel.

'Oh, and I guess I'll stay at the Grosvenor, as usual,' he appended, as if reading her thoughts. 'Unless you'd prefer me to stay here.'

To stay here!

Maggie swallowed a little convulsively, and then felt an enormous sense of relief when she heard a door slam downstairs. She was almost sure Mrs Lewis had left, and she prayed that it was Lindsey. Not just because she was anxious about her daughter's whereabouts, but because it would enable her to avoid an awkward response.

Neil had heard the slamming door too, and he swung his legs off the sofa and got to his feet. They both stood, like two statues, waiting for the sitting room door to open, but as if to confound their expectations Lindsey didn't pause on the first landing, but continued on up to her room.

'Hell!'

Ignoring Maggie's admonition to wait, he strode across to the door and swung it open. 'Lindsey,' he called, keeping the edge out of his voice with evident difficulty, 'd'you want to come down and say hello?'

'Daddy!'

There was no doubting Lindsey's delight at Neil's appearance, and Maggie heard her clatter down the stairs again and throw herself into his arms. As she stood in the sitting room, trying to remember how long it was since Lindsey had embraced her with such enthusiasm, she heard her daughter chattering, asking Neil what he was doing in London, and whether he'd come especially to see her.

'What else, princess?' Maggie overheard his reply and the exuberant response she gave him. 'It's been far too long since we spent any time together. You haven't even seen my new house.'

Maggie sensed Lindsey detaching herself. 'Haversham?' She paused. 'Oh, yes, Mum said you'd moved. Is it nice?'

Nice? Maggie grimaced. 'Nice' was such an inadequate word to describe Neil's renovation of Haversham House.

'I think so,' he said now. 'You'd better come and see for yourself. I don't think your mother got to see it, but there's a gym, and poolhouse, and a sauna.'

'Really?' Lindsey was evidently impressed. Then she said, 'No. Mum didn't say much about the house at all. Just that she was surprised you needed so much space.'

Maggie hadn't said that, and she started forward, intending to deny it. But then it dawned on her that it had probably been Mike Reynolds who had made that comment. It must gall him to know that Neil had used his money so much more shrewdly than himself.

'You can never have too much space,' Neil remarked now, his hand around her wrist, pulling her after him into the sitting room. 'Here is your mother,' he added unnecessarily. 'I believe she's got a message for you.'

As if he couldn't have given it to her himself, thought Maggie, half-resentfully, even though she guessed Neil was trying to maintain his good relationship with his daughter. 'Um—yes,' she said, meeting Lindsey's unfriendly eyes defensively. 'Mike called. He said to tell you he'll be away for a few days, and that he'll phone you when he gets back.'

'Away?' There was no doubting Lindsey's disappointment now, and, releasing her wrist from her father, she rubbed it with an absent hand. 'Did he say where he was going?' she added, after a moment. 'Damn, I wanted to tell him Daddy was here. He so much wanted to see you, for you and him to be friends again.'

Meeting her ex-husband's eyes, Maggie had no doubt that there was no way Neil and Mike Reynolds could ever 'be friends again'. Not that he said so, of course. He was far too aware of the pitfalls for that.

'I don't believe that was discussed,' he offered now, dragging his gaze from Maggie's with a scarcely perceptible shrug in her direction. 'Never mind. It gives us an opportunity to spend some time together. Why don't you come back with me to Haversham for a few days?'

Maggie stifled a gasp behind her hand, but Lindsey had no such reservations. 'To Haversham!' she exclaimed. 'You want me to go all the way to Northumberland! Get real, Daddy, I'm in school. I can't just abandon my education.'

'Why not?' Neil's dark brows arched now, and Maggie sensed the reproof before it was voiced. 'I understand you've been thinking of leaving school altogether. Or did you intend to work in Bournemouth in your spare time?'

Lindsey's accusing gaze was turned on her mother. 'Who told you? Aunt Jackie? She swore she wouldn't.'

Maggie shrugged. 'How did you expect to keep it a secret?' she asked impatiently. 'I am half-owner of the shop, you know.'

'It was just a bit of fun.' Lindsey looked sulky now. 'I never expected to get the job.'

Or perhaps she'd hoped she might, because she was her mother's daughter, thought Maggie ruefully. And if the manageress at the Bournemouth shop had been taking the interviews instead of Jackie she might have got away with it as well.

'Anyway, that's not important,' put in Neil placatingly. 'I'm sure your headmistress wouldn't object if you took just a couple of days off school next week. I'll ring her, if you like.' He grinned. 'I'm good with older women. And I seem to remember she is a little bit more elderly than me.'

Lindsey's lips twitched. 'You're not elderly,' she said, reluctantly responding to his magnetic charm. Ten years ago, girls of her age had worshipped him at every concert he'd given. Every album he'd released had gone platinum; every single had topped the charts. Was it any wonder that he could charm his daughter? Maggie wondered wryly. But would it be enough to make Lindsey his willing slave?

'So how about it?' he pressed, exchanging a significant look with Maggie. 'Your mother can come along too. When she came up last weekend, it was just a flying visit. I think she looks tired. The break would do you both good.'

CHAPTER SEVEN

SHE should have refused to come.

Staring out at the bleak countryside beyond the car's windows, Maggie acknowledged that she had complied with Neil's wishes far too easily.

But his suggestion of bringing Lindsey here, of getting her far away from London, and the influence Mike Reynolds found much too easy to exploit, had seemed irresistible, and she'd been afraid to refuse the invitation for herself too strongly, for fear of rocking the boat.

Well, that was her excuse anyway, Maggie reflected, wondering what Nicola Braithwaite would think when they turned up at Neil's door again. She couldn't believe Nicola had been a party to it, and she was probably inviting a whole lot of unnecessary heartache, when if she'd stuck to her guns Lindsey would eventually have agreed to go without her.

After all, it wasn't as if she and her daughter were inseparable. Since the affair with Mike Reynolds, Lindsey had seemed to be doing her best to drive them apart. But curiously enough she had been strangely eager that her mother should go with them, and Maggie hoped she wasn't nurturing any false hopes that she and Neil might get together again.

In addition to which, as if to confound her father's hopes, she had spent a good part of the journey asking him about Mike. She'd been too young when Neil had split from his agent to remember any acrimony between them, and her opinion of their break-up was based on what the other man had told her.

Of course, Mike had been too astute to attempt to denigrate her father. The version of the breakdown in their working relationship he had fed Linsey, and which she had spent the journey repeating to her father, bore all the hall-marks of a major whitewashing job. Neil had become too successful, Mike had told her ruefully. He'd forgotten who his friends were when his career had taken off. All he wanted was a chance to redress the balance. It would mean such a lot to him, she said, if Neil would help him out.

From her seat in the back of the Mercedes—her choice; she had no desire to encourage Lindsey's possible misconceptions about her relationship with her ex-husband—Maggie had to admire Neil for the patience he showed towards his daughter. He didn't get angry with her, or contradict her, or say anything to change her opinion of the man she professed to love. But, equally, he didn't endorse her sentiments, or make any comments beyond those that politeness demanded.

And eventually—probably as Neil had hoped, Maggie acknowledged irritably—Lindsey got tired of the virtually one-sided conversation. But, whereas she might have accused Maggie of being deliberately obstructive, she was sufficiently fond—or in awe—of her father that she didn't demur. Or perhaps she was wary of rocking the boat too, thought Maggie cynically. Lindsey knew Neil had made the journey south to see her. She must believe he was considering doing what Mike had asked.

She was probably right, mused Maggie wearily, feeling the weight of her own misgivings bearing down on her yet again. Jackie thought she was mad for coming here, and who could blame her? And she didn't know the half of it, Maggie conceded with a sigh.

Beyond Scotch Corner, the dual carriageway was optimistically labelled a motorway. It was still a two-lane road, but now there were no exits on the right. Early on a Saturday afternoon, the traffic was still fairly heavy, heading for the Mecca of the Gateshead Metro Centre, but at least there were signs for Newcastle now, and Maggie knew they were about forty miles from their destination.

They'd stopped for lunch at a motorway service area on the M1. Lindsey had ploughed her way through the all-day breakfast, but all Maggie had managed was a sandwich and some coffee. Neil, meanwhile, had tucked into fish and chips, clearly demonstrating his detachment from any doubts she might be feeling.

It was getting dark by the time they turned onto the A69. The sky had been fairly grey since they left London, and now a few shreds of sleet drifted against the windscreen. The clouds looked thick enough for snow, thought Maggie, feeling a renewal of tension. How would Lindsey react if she was confined to the house?

'We don't have too much farther to go, do we?' Lindsey asked, peering through the window. 'We always came by train or plane before.' She looked at her father. 'Why did you decide to drive down?'

'I like driving,' said Neil carelessly. 'And I might not have been able to persuade your mother to join us if I hadn't brought the car.'

Maggie's eyes widened, but before she could make any scathing retort about the way she had been put on the spot Lindsey intervened. 'Yes,' she said. 'And that would have been a pity. I think she needs to get away from Aunt Jackie. Without her influence, Mum wouldn't spend half so much time at the office.'

'*Lindsey!*'

'Your mother works long hours, does she?'

As Maggie had expected, this was one subject on which her daughter and her ex-husband would obviously agree.

'You'd better believe it,' agreed Lindsey fervently, as if her mother weren't sitting right behind them. 'We used to have fun together, but these days she's always too busy to make time for me.'

'That's not true!'

Maggie had told herself she would not be provoked, but that was too close to the bone. If she and Lindsey didn't spend as much time together as they used to, it wasn't all her fault.

'It is true,' declared Lindsey, glancing over her shoulder, and Maggie wondered if she was taking out the frustration she felt with her father's monosyllabic answers on her. 'How long is it since we went shopping together? Can you remember the last time we went to see a show, or had a meal at a restaurant, without you and Aunt Jackie talking shop?'

Maggie was silenced. It was true that when she and Lindsey had gone out for a meal she had usually asked Jackie to join them. But that was because she felt sorry for her sister, who had no family of her own, and also because she thought Lindsey liked her to come along, because her mother was such boring company.

'I thought you liked Aunt Jackie,' remarked Neil now, and Maggie waited somewhat apprehensively for Lindsey's reply.

'Well, I did,' muttered Lindsey unwillingly. 'Until she started telling me things I didn't want to know.' She lifted her shoulders in a dismissing gesture. 'It doesn't matter now. Oh—there's the George. I remember that.'

Maggie set her jaw in some frustration herself now. Neil was answering Lindsey, reminding his daughter of when she had last visited here some twenty months ago, and there was no way Maggie could resurrect the subject of her sister without sounding as if she believed what Lindsey had said. Of course, there could be a fairly innocent explanation. Jackie could have been endorsing her mother's complaints about Mike Reynolds, and Lindsey had objected to her being involved. Yes, that was probably what it was, Maggie assured herself. What else could Jackie have told her, for heaven's sake?

The drive gates were open, and the Mercedes swept between them with barely a pause. Then the rhododendron hedge enveloped the car and they sped swiftly up the roadway to the house.

Maggie hadn't expected Lindsey to be impressed with Haversham House, but she was. Her first exclamation, as she got out of the car, was a forerunner of the enthusiasm she expressed when they got inside. 'Gosh,' she breathed as they entered the warmth of the entrance hall, 'I never expected anything like this.' She swung around, taking in the fieldstone fireplace, where a pile of locally cut logs burnt brightly, the tiled floor, spread with thick, jewel-patterned rugs, and the elegant fan of the staircase, which led to the gallery upstairs. 'It's fantastic! Don't you think so, Mum?'

'I think your mother's tired,' put in Neil, before Maggie could answer, and she was subjecting him to an angry glare when Mrs Fenwick appeared from the kitchen.

'Hello again, Ms Freeman,' she said. 'Did you have a good journey? Oh, and this must be your daughter. She looks a lot like you.'

'She's Neil's daughter too,' said Maggie, a little stiffly, wondering if he had explained the relationship. 'Um—am I staying in the same room as before, Mrs Fenwick? I think I'd like to freshen up, if you don't mind?'

Mrs Fenwick looked enquiringly at her employer, and with some impatience Neil inclined his head. 'But I had hoped you'd like to look around a bit, before you go and change, Maggie. I want to show Lindsey the recreation suite, and I thought you might be interested too.'

'Some other time,' said Maggie, refusing to be influenced by the fact that Lindsey was expecting her to give in. 'You go ahead,' she said to her daughter. 'I'll see you both later.' Her lips tightened meaningfully. 'After I've had a rest.'

Two could play at that game, she thought crossly as she eschewed Mrs Fenwick's help with her suitcase and made her way upstairs. She was in no mood to listen to Lindsey's paeans of praise for Neil's home, particularly when her admiration was so obviously misplaced. She suspected Lindsey thought she was being clever, raving about the beauty of her father's house. Perhaps she thought if she flattered him enough he might be more inclined to humour her, though, knowing Neil as she did, Maggie doubted she would have any success.

In any event, it wasn't her problem, Maggie decided dourly. It was quite a relief to leave the negotiation to Neil. And if, by bringing her here, he thought to provide himself with an ally he was going to learn that he couldn't automatically count on her support.

Nevertheless, soaking in the bath some thirty minutes later, Maggie had to admit that being here wasn't all bad. She did seem to spend a lot of time working these days,

and the prospect of taking a break from her worries did
have some appeal, despite her surroundings. But she would
still argue that her relationship with Lindsey had not suffered because of her work. Her daughter had certainly never
given her the impression that she was pining for her company.

But how could she tell? Sinking lower into the bath,
Maggie rested her head against the rim and expelled a
weary sigh. The problem of Lindsey just wouldn't go away,
and she closed her eyes against the constant barrage of her
thoughts.

The sound of a door slamming close at hand brought her
upright with a jerk. She hadn't forgotten what had happened the last time she'd fallen asleep in this bath, and her
eyes turned apprehensively towards the bathroom door,
which she had deliberately locked against intruders.

'Mum!' Lindsey's voice caused the hairs on the back of
her neck to subside again. 'Mum, are you in there? Can I
come in?'

'Wait a minute.' Dripping water in all directions, Maggie
stepped out onto the padded mat beside the bath, grabbing
a towel from the heated rail to wrap around her. Then,
regretting the necessity, she ran across the tiled floor to
release the lock, hurrying back to the bath again before
calling, 'Come in.'

'Was the door locked?' asked Lindsey in surprise as her
mother immersed herself again in the warm water. 'I don't
think you need to worry. I don't think any of Daddy's staff
would invade your privacy.'

How about Daddy himself? Maggie asked silently, wondering what Lindsey would say if she told her what had
happened the last time she was here. She probably wouldn't
believe it, conceded Maggie ruefully. In their children's
eyes, parents didn't do that sort of thing.

'I suppose it's just habit,' she responded now, looking
up at her daughter with enquiring eyes. 'Well? Did you see
the recreation area?'

'Did I!'

Lindsey's enthusiasm hadn't waned, and Maggie could
only assume Neil was a better salesperson than she was. In

the past few years, when she'd suggested Lindsey ought to go and stay with her father, she'd always found an excuse for refusing. But now it seemed she was completely overwhelmed by her surroundings.

'The pool is huge,' Lindsey continued, perching on the edge of the bath and trailing a finger in the bubbly water. 'There's a hot tub, too, and a sauna, and the gym has every kind of exercise equipment imaginable.'

Maggie arched brows that were several shades darker then her hair. 'It sounds impressive.'

'It is.' Lindsey sighed. 'I just wish it was nearer to London. I mean, I'd like to spend more time with Daddy, but him being up here doesn't make it easy.'

Maggie managed not to show any emotion. But it was hard to hide her feelings at the realisation that Lindsey had completed several whole sentences without mentioning Mike Reynolds' name once. She wasn't stupid. She knew that that small victory might not mean a thing. But the fact remained that Neil had achieved what she would have thought was the impossible. He had made Lindsey think for herself again, instead of just parroting what Mike Reynolds said.

'Well, you'll have to take advantage of it while you're here,' Maggie declared, reaching for a facecloth and beginning to soap her arms. She viewed her daughter's jean-clad figure. 'Are you changing before supper?'

Lindsey frowned, looking down at her appearance with less interest. 'Do you think I should?' she asked, her tone a little grudging. 'There's only going to be Daddy and Luke Parry to impress.'

'I'm not suggesting you try to impress anyone,' murmured Maggie carefully, 'but as you travelled up in those clothes you might want to freshen up.' She paused. 'Um—did your father actually say there's only to be the four of us for supper?'

Lindsey met her mother's cautious gaze. 'Who else could there be?' she asked. And then, a light dawning behind her eyes, she said, 'Oh, God, you don't mean Daddy's invited Mike to join us?'

'No.' Maggie cursed herself for being so ambiguous, but

she couldn't withdraw her statement now. 'I—I believe your father has a girlfriend. I met her when I was here last weekend.'

'A girlfriend?' Although Maggie might have regretted having to bring the subject up, there was no denying it briefly erased the thought of Mike Reynolds from Lindsey's mind. 'Who is she? Where does she live? Do I know her?'

'You might—remember her,' said Maggie, glad she could use the excuse of washing her legs to avoid her daughter's eyes. 'Her name's Nicola—Braithwaite. But she used to be Nicola Armstrong before she was married.'

'She's married!'

Although Maggie was concentrating on not saying anything controversial, she was amused at the censure in her daughter's voice. It was funny, she thought, how young people could be so moral when it came to the older generation, while ignoring such distinctions in their own lives.

'She's divorced,' she replied, hoping to evade any further explanations. 'Now—I think you'd better go and let me get finished. You might not have to worry about what you look like, but I'm afraid I do.'

'Why?' Lindsey got up from the bath and regarded her mother critically. 'You look good whatever you wear. Just because you're older than me, it doesn't mean you're not attractive. I'm sure Daddy thinks so, whatever his relationship with this Braithwaite woman might be.'

Maggie's lips tightened. 'Don't bet on it,' she remarked, barely audibly, but Lindsey heard her.

'Why not?' she countered. ''Daddy may have walked out but he wasn't the one who got bored with the marriage, you were. Aunt Jackie said so. I sometimes wonder what it was you were looking for.'

So do I, reflected Maggie cynically, but she didn't say it. The last thing she wanted was Lindsey trying to play matchmaker between her and Neil. Apart from anything else, that wasn't why they were here. But she intended to speak to Jackie when they got back. She would not have her putting ideas into Lindsey's head.

'We all make mistakes,' she said at last, hoping her daughter would make the connection and go.

But all Lindsey said was, 'I'm glad you realise it was a mistake,' and disappeared out the door before Maggie could correct her.

At least she hadn't had to come down to supper in the clothes she had travelled in, thought Maggie later as she descended the impressive staircase to the hall below. The black silk jersey dress she was wearing would bear comparison with anything Nicola Braithwaite might wear, the skirt flaring from the hips, and ending just above the knee. The fact that it drew attention to the sheer black stockings that covered her long legs was deliberate. She might have put on a few inches, she conceded honestly, but her legs were still as shapely as before.

She heard Lindsey's voice as she walked across the hall to the drawing room. Her daughter sounded more animated than she had for some time and the source of the laughter that punctuated her speech was explained by Luke Parry's familiar presence.

'The damn horse kept turning round,' he said, 'and there was my foot still stuck in the stirrup. No wonder I twisted my knee! I'm lucky he didn't take off across the yard.'

Lindsey was giggling again as Maggie appeared in the doorway, and she turned to her mother with dancing eyes. 'Luke's just been telling me how he hurt his leg,' she said. 'He says he'll take me out tomorrow. Is that OK?'

Maggie made a helpless gesture. 'If that's what you want,' she said, looking to Luke. 'And if he doesn't mind.'

'I'll look forward to it,' said Luke cheerfully. 'It's time Lindsey got up on a horse again.'

'You mean—you'll take her riding?' exclaimed Maggie, not having understood before, and Lindsey gave her an impatient look.

'What else?' she said. 'Oh, Mum, you didn't think I meant in the Land Rover, did you?'

'I suppose I did.' Maggie came farther into the room, and accepted the glass of sherry Luke poured for her. She shrugged. 'You don't have any gear.'

'She can borrow a hat,' said Luke, 'and a pair of jeans

and a warm jacket are good enough.' He looked at Lindsey.
'You have some boots, don't you?'

'Sure.' Lindsey shrugged, raising her own glass of white
wine to her lips. She grimaced. 'Mum is just hyper-anxious.
She doesn't believe I can look after myself.'

Which was probably true, conceded Maggie, going to
warm her hands at the fire. But at least her daughter had
taken some trouble with her appearance too. Although she
was wearing trousers, they were a silk pair Maggie had
bought her at Christmas, and the skinny top she was wearing with them exposed the slender column of her neck.

'Are we—that is—is there just to be us for supper?' she
asked Luke as she came to join her, and he gave her a wary
look.

'I believe so,' he acknowledged. 'Unless Neil gave you
the impression that—'

'He didn't,' Maggie interrupted him quickly as the man
himself came into the room. The last thing she wanted was
for Neil to think she'd been asking questions about him.
Her eyes were drawn to the couch, as if by a magnet, and
she couldn't get the image of what had happened there out
of her mind.

'Hi, Daddy.'

Lindsey's greeting was a welcome diversion, and Maggie
told herself to forget what had happened before, and concentrate on what was happening now. For her daughter's
sake, she had to behave normally, and that meant treating
Neil like an old friend, not an enemy.

If he approved of the effort she had made with her appearance, he didn't say so. Lindsey had captured his attention, and apart from a slight nod of acknowledgement towards herself and Luke Neil spent the time before supper
talking to his daughter. The fact that she was telling him
about Luke's suggestion that they go riding the following
day made Maggie's feelings of isolation somewhat ridiculous. But she couldn't help the sense of being excluded that
their being together evoked.

Their relationship was unmistakable. Although Lindsey
wasn't as tall as Neil, she had her father's build and easy
grace of movement. In addition to which, their colouring

was identical, Lindsey's thick dark hair a mirror of her father's.

'It's good to see Lindsey here again,' Luke commented at her elbow, and she guessed the other man was aware of her misgivings.

'Yes, isn't it?' she said bravely, determined not to sound envious. 'Um—how's the foal?'

Luke frowned. 'What foal?'

Maggie was discomfited. 'The *foal*,' she said unhappily, forgetting that that particular morning would have retained no significance in his mind. She coloured. 'The foal Nicola—Braithwaite had come to see the morning I left.'

'Oh, *that* foal!' exclaimed Luke, and Maggie could have melted with embarrassment. 'We called him Midnight, by the way. Perhaps you'd like to see him too?'

'Perhaps,' murmured Maggie noncommittally, wishing she'd never asked, and as she turned away to take a sip of her drink she saw Neil looking her way. Oh, yes, he'd heard, she thought impatiently, wondering why she'd let herself in for this. The way Lindsey was behaving, her being here was totally unnecessary.

They ate in the dining room, as before, and Lindsey had no qualms about saying what she thought. 'It reminds me of one of those stately homes,' she said. 'The kind they write about in women's magazines.' She grimaced. 'Not the kind of magazines Mum used to appear in, but I think she'd have looked pretty good draped over one of those squashy sofas in the other room, or coming down the stairs in a sexy negligée. What do you think, Daddy?'

Maggie wished the floor would open up and swallow her. It was bad enough that Lindsey should have made a distinction between a woman's magazine and the kind of magazine she used to model for. For heaven's sake, she hadn't been an artist's model, just someone who looked good in expensive clothes. The glossy pages she had graced had appeared in fashion magazines and catalogues, not *Penthouse* or *Playboy*, as her daughter had seemed to imply. But as well as that she had invited her father's opinion, and, not knowing the whole story, she was making things worse. What was she trying to do? Effect a reconciliation?

Or divert Neil's attention from Mike Reynolds and the obvious threat he posed?

Either way, Maggie wished she would leave her out of it, especially when Neil met her gaze with a wry expression. Dear God, surely he didn't think she had put Lindsey up to this? She glared at him, trying to convey the fact that she was appalled by their daughter's remark.

'I think Maggie would look good anywhere,' declared Luke gallantly, defusing the situation. 'Have you ever thought about modelling, Lindsey? Or are you the academic one of the family?'

'Actually, I want to get married,' declared Lindsey at once, and Maggie acknowledged that there were worse things than being embarrassed. 'I don't want a career; I want to have lots of babies. I've always wanted a brother or a sister, but Mum was never interested in raising a family.'

CHAPTER EIGHT

'WHO told you that?'

The words were out before Maggie could stop them, and she cursed herself for caring one way or the other. It had to have been Neil. There was no one else involved. Which made her glad that Lindsey had stopped visiting her father on a regular basis.

'It was Aunt Jackie, actually,' said Lindsey, regarding her mother defensively. 'She said that's why you and she opened the boutiques. Then—well, you and Daddy split up, and it wasn't a possibility after that.'

Maggie swallowed her indignation. 'I expect Jackie meant well,' she responded, managing a tight smile in Neil's direction, but she was grateful that Mrs Fenwick arrived at that moment to clear the pudding plates, and of the fact that she had at least enjoyed the meal before Lindsey had chosen to intervene.

Coffee was again served in the drawing room, and, perhaps because she was aware that she had been rather indiscreet earlier, Lindsey chose to spend the rest of the evening flicking through old issues of *Horse and Hound*. It was as if she had just remembered what she was doing here, and even her attitude towards her father was subdued.

Meanwhile Maggie had to put up with Neil sprawling on the couch beside her. Although she would have preferred to sit beside Luke, as before, Lindsey had beaten her to it, and it was difficult to relax with Neil's muscled thigh a scant few inches from hers.

Had he sat there deliberately? she wondered. There were plenty of other chairs about the room. Did he want her to remember what had happened? Wasn't it enough for him that she had made a fool of herself yet again?

'How is Jackie?' Neil asked, when Luke's rambling monologue about the problems of rearing foals in cold weather finally faltered to a halt, and Maggie forced herself to reply in an equally casual vein.

'She's fine,' she said, convinced that he wasn't really interested. He and Jackie had never hit it off, even in the days when Jackie's husband had been around.

'She didn't marry again?'

Now she was certain he was just baiting her. 'No,' she said. 'Why would she want to do that?'

'Indeed.' His tone was mocking. 'She's something of a feminist, isn't she? I'm surprised she let you come here. Isn't she afraid I might corrupt you again?'

Maggie's lips tightened. 'That's hardly likely, is it?' she retorted shortly, aware that Lindsey was listening to what they said.

'Oh, I don't know.' Neil's tone was tormenting. 'And she doesn't know that.' He paused. 'Or does she? Do you still tell her everything you do?'

'I never told her everything I did,' retorted Maggie, flashing a warning look in their daughter's direction. She turned back to Luke, desperate for a diversion. 'You said Barbara was married again; where is she living? I expect the twins are quite grown-up.'

She knew she shouldn't have asked about Barbara. The last time she'd brought the subject up, there'd been a definite atmosphere afterwards, and it had only been her eagerness to escape Neil's mocking tongue that had driven her to ask what she had.

'As a matter of fact, she married an American, and they live in Boston,' replied Luke tautly. 'I only see the boys about once a year.'

'Which is more than I've seen you lately, brat,' put in Neil, in an obvious effort to reassure his friend. 'Your mother says you prefer staying in London. That's not much of a compliment to me.'

'Oh.' Lindsey looked up from the magazine she was supposed to be reading. 'You know why. There's nothing to do here—and you're always working. Besides, I've got a social life in town.'

Neil shrugged. 'You could have a social life here.'

Lindsey pulled a face. 'Can you see Mike leaving London for me?'

'He might. If he really cares about you,' remarked her father mildly. 'There is life after London, I can vouch for that.'

'Oh, no.' Lindsey put her magazine aside and got to her feet. 'I know what you're trying to do. You think that if I ask Mike to move up here and he refuses I'll immediately think he doesn't care about me. Well, forget it, Daddy. Mike's business is in London. If you want to see more of me, you'll have to move back to town.'

Maggie drew a breath. Although she was disappointed with Lindsey's answer, she couldn't say she was surprised. And it was something of a coup to see Neil dealing with this set-back. Until then, she'd been sure he'd thought she was exaggerating the problem.

'Anyway, I'm tired,' said Lindsey, evidently not prepared to continue the discussion. 'If you don't mind, I'll go and watch television in bed.'

'By my guest,' said Neil drily, still nursing his resentment, and Lindsey bent to kiss her mother's cheek before leaving the room.

'That's my cue,' said Luke, as he had done on that other occasion, but this time Maggie had no intention of being left with Neil.

'And me,' she said, even though it was barely nine-thirty. 'Goodnight.' She included both of them in a polite smile, and started after her daughter.

'Wait a minute.' Neil got to his feet as Luke, too, started for the door. 'Don't you think we ought to talk, Maggie? This is an opportunity. Or are you so peeved that I brought you here that you're prepared to ignore the problem?'

'I'm not peeved that you brought me here,' said Maggie, between her teeth, and Luke made an awkward salute of farewell.

'Well, look, you can do without me,' he said, edging past

her. 'I'll see you in the morning, Maggie. Perhaps you'd like to join Lindsey and me on our ride.'

'I wish you'd stay, Luke,' said Maggie, in lieu of answering his invitation. She had no desire to spend the rest of the evening fencing with her ex-husband.

'Let him go,' ordered Neil, and Luke gave her a rueful grimace. 'This isn't Luke's problem. It's ours.'

'So you accept that it's a problem now?'

'Maggie!'

'I'm out of here,' put in Luke, not wanting any further argument. 'See you both in the morning.' He pulled a wry face. 'I hope.'

With the door closed behind him, Maggie was left in the ignominious position of not knowing what to do for the best. It would be easy enough to open the door again and do as she'd intended and leave, but if Neil really wanted to talk ought she to stop him? She sighed, resting her hands on the back of the sofa and attempting to face her ex-husband with equanimity. But she knew he thought she was afraid of being alone with him, and although that might be true she owed it to herself not to show it.

'Well?' she said at last, when it was obvious he didn't intend to make it easy for her. 'What is it you want to say?'

'Come and sit down.'

Maggie held up her head. 'So you can make a fool of me again? I don't think so.'

'I'm not in the mood to make a fool of anyone,' retorted Neil, his expression revealing his irritation. 'For God's sake, Maggie, its not my fault that you came on to me like a frustrated spinster! How was I to know you were that desperate for a man?'

'I'm going to bed!'

Maggie reached for the handle of the door and jerked it open. Her hands were trembling, but the mortification she was feeling inside was a hundred times worse than that. He'd done it again, she thought. Only he'd used his tongue this time to humiliate her. She never learned, she chided herself angrily. She just let him go on crucifying her.

'Wait—' He caught her before she started up the stairs, his hand, circling her upper arm, preventing her from going on. 'I'm sorry,' he muttered, his face in the firelight dark and somehow entreating. 'You hurt me, Maggie. Don't blame me if sometimes I can't help letting it show.'

Maggie swallowed. 'Do you expect me to believe that?'

Neil's eyes darkened. 'How would you have felt if you'd found out I'd been having an affair with another woman?'

'I wasn't having an affair—'

'We won't go into that.' Neil still wouldn't talk about it. 'The fact is, you slept with Massey. And that's something I've never been able to forgive.'

'Neil—'

'Come back,' he said, ignoring her plea. 'Please. Surely we can talk about our daughter without prejudice?'

Maggie drew her arm free. 'You promise not to take advantage of me?'

Neil's lips twisted. 'What's that supposed to mean?'

'It means we talk about Lindsey, and nothing else,' replied Maggie. 'Otherwise I might as well go to bed now.'

Neil stepped back, a silent but eloquent gesture of his compliance, and despite her misgivings Maggie preceded him back into the drawing room. Neil closed the door, and then, observing how she had seated herself in the middle of one of the sofas, took the other, regarding her with cool appraisal across the width of the hearth.

'OK,' he said, and she breathed a little more easily at this evidence of his sincerity, 'I accept that Lindsey's infatuated with the—with Reynolds. Obviously—' He paused here. 'Obviously, she likes what he's doing for her. What we have to decide is how to handle what comes next.'

Maggie frowned. 'What will come next?'

'Well...' Neil was thoughtful '...if I know Mike, he's not going to give up at the first obstacle.'

'What obstacle?'

'Me,' said Neil heavily. 'The fact that I'm not going to do what the bastard wants. In his shoes, I'd have to have a contingency plan, and my guess is that he'll suggest that they get engaged.'

'You're joking!'

'Do you think so?' Neil's expression was depressingly

unconvinced. 'It's his only obvious option, if he wants to get a result.'

Maggie groaned. 'Oh, God!'

'Of course, he must believe that I'll never let him marry her,' added Neil broodingly, staring at his balled fists with a savage expression. 'He must have been really choked when he realised his initial plan hadn't worked.'

'Well, he was angry,' Maggie admitted. 'But what do you mean—you wouldn't condone their marriage, would you?' Her breath caught in her throat. 'Not with him!'

Neil gave her a brief but chilling look. 'No,' he said, as if it were necessary to explain himself. 'But Reynolds can't be sure of that, can he? If we can make him believe it's not going to change my mind, he may give up.'

Maggie looked doubtful. 'Do you believe that?'

'No.' Neil sighed. 'But I'm trying to take an optimistic view.'

Maggie's lips twisted. 'I wish I could.'

'Well, we know he's in financial difficulties, don't we?'

'I suppose so.'

'Take my word for it. He's got debts in excess of some six hundred thousand pounds. I had a friend of mine check him out, so the figures aren't exaggerated. The way I hear it, his creditors are breathing down his neck.'

Maggie gulped. 'Six hundred thousand pounds!'

'And the rest,' agreed Neil grimly, gazing into the smouldering fire. 'That's only the scum that's floated to the top of the pond. My guess is that there's probably another half million hidden underneath.'

Maggie was shocked. Mike Reynolds' debts made even her overdraft look respectable. 'And—and if he doesn't—give up?' she ventured tentatively. 'What then?'

'Then—I guess it's up to me to buy him off,' said Neil flatly. 'And I don't mean by getting involved in the music scene again, like he suggested. Somehow I'll find a way to liquidate some of my assets. I'll do whatever I can to get that swine off Lindsey's back.'

Maggie felt an enormous sense of relief. 'Oh, Neil—'

'Don't look at me like that,' he commanded harshly, and she thought for a moment he was warning her off. Her face suffused with unwanted colour, and a denial trembled on her lips. But before she could voice it he explained, 'It may not work.'

She blinked. 'What do you mean?'

He got to his feet and approached the hearth, resting one foot on the brass fender and looking down at her with sardonic eyes. 'I mean we're assuming Lindsey won't object to our plans.' His brow arched mockingly. 'Something tells me it might not be that simple.'

'But surely she'd realise—?'

'What?'

'Well, that you were buying him off.'

'Perhaps.' Neil removed his foot from the fender and turned so that his back was to the fire. 'But she thinks she's in love with him. You told me they were lovers.'

'They were. They *are*.' Maggie was amazed at how embarrassed she felt discussing such things with her ex-husband. And the fact that he was towering over her now didn't help at all. 'I'm sure when she realises he's only using her—'

'Physically using her, you mean?' suggested Neil politely, and Maggie took a nervous breath.

'To get to you,' she amended firmly. She cast a brief glance up at him. 'Well, if that's settled, I think I'll go to bed.'

'Nothing's settled,' declared Neil, when she would have risen to her feet, and she subsided again with some apprehension. 'We're just having a discussion.' He paused, and she had the uneasy feeling that he was considering how to voice his next words. 'Um—I also had my—colleague check out The Frock Shops. It seems you and your sister are still waiting to make your first million, too.'

His audacity stunned her. 'You did *what*?'

'I wanted to know what contribution you might be prepared to make should this business with Reynolds need financing,' he remarked mildly. 'Unfortunately, it seems The Frock Shops are struggling for their survival.'

'That's not true!' Maggie sprang to her feet now, uncaring that by doing so she put herself that much nearer to his mocking face. 'There's been a recession, Neil. Or didn't you know that, sitting up here in your ivory tower? All small businesses are struggling for their survival. But we'll make it. Don't you worry about that.'

'So your coming here that first time had nothing to do with you needing a loan yourself?' he countered, not at all put out by her aggression, and Maggie seethed.

'No, it did not,' she denied furiously. 'I wouldn't take anything from you. I think I told you that before.'

'Well, you did,' conceded Neil evenly, his dark gaze disturbingly intent. 'Forgive me if I find it hard to believe. I can't think of any other reason why you might want to get into my bed.'

Maggie's mouth dropped. 'You promised you wouldn't bring that up again.'

'I lied.'

'You're despicable!'

'No. Just curious.'

Maggie steeled herself not to be intimidated by his deliberate sarcasm. 'It was the wine,' she said curtly. 'As you implied, I must have been mad to allow you to touch me. I'm usually much more fastidious.'

A muscle in Neil's cheek jerked. 'I wouldn't say that.'

The urge to slap his mocking face was almost overwhelming, but this time she was determined not to let him see he could hurt her. 'You can say what you like,' she declared tersely. 'So long as I have the same privilege.'

Neil tilted his head. 'What's that supposed to mean? I haven't noticed you being particularly reticent in your criticisms of me.'

Maggie managed an innocent look. 'Oh, I wasn't thinking of you,' she remarked. 'I was thinking of Mrs Braithwaite. I wonder if she realises how much you enjoy baiting your wife?'

'Ex-wife,' said Neil, with a little less tolerance, and Maggie knew she had touched a nerve.

'Ex-wife, then,' she conceded, lifting her shoulders carelessly. 'You know, Neil, some people might think you were still attracted to me.'

'But we know different, don't we?' he snapped, definitely nettled now, and Maggie hid a small smile.

'Do we?' she countered, enjoying the reversal of their positions. 'How do I know you weren't fighting the urge to give in?'

'We know,' said Neil grimly, and before she could guess his intention he had grabbed her hand and forced it against his groin. 'Now do you believe me?' he snapped, glaring at her with real loathing. 'As far as I'm concerned, you're poison. And I don't have any urge to contaminate myself again.'

Maggie stared back, unwilling to give up her advantage so easily, and, as she did so, something unexpected happened. Beneath her fingers she felt him hardening, and with a muffled oath he thrust her hand away.

'Get out of here,' he snarled, swinging round to face the fire. With his hands braced on the mantel, he had his back to her now, and although she'd felt that stirring of his flesh for herself she was quite prepared to believe he hated her at that moment. 'Go to bed,' he added. 'You make me sick!'

Maggie swallowed. 'Neil—'

'I said, go to bed!'

'I know you did, only—'

'Only? Only what?' Almost wearily, it seemed, he turned to face her again, and it took an enormous effort of will-power not to let her eyes slip below the level of his waist. 'Only you can't let it go, can you, Maggie?' he demanded scornfully. 'You think you've scored some kind of victory, and you've got to savour it to the full.'

'No—'

'Yes.' With a gesture of defeat, he walked to the sofa where he had been sitting earlier and flung himself full-length on the cushions. 'OK,' he said. 'If that's what you want, who am I to argue? It's one way of expunging my frustration.' His hand moved to his belt, and he unloosened the buckle with provocative ease. 'By the way,' he added, 'I hope you've got some protection. I'm afraid I haven't come prepared.'

Maggie gasped. 'You can't think—' she began, only to have him interrupt her again.

'Oh, yes, I think,' he told her harshly, releasing the but-

ton at his waist. 'It's what you've been wanting ever since
you got here. You've got some crazy notion in your head
that this is why I came down to London—to bring you
back. Why else would you take so much trouble over your
appearance? Unless you were hoping to impress Luke, of
course.'

Maggie was almost speechless. Any satisfaction she
might have felt at him noticing how she looked was totally
eclipsed by his blatant arrogance. She could hardly defend
herself by saying that her efforts had been made in case
Nicola Braithwaite had been invited to join them. Why
should she care what Nicola thought of her appearance?
Why should she try to compete, when Neil was the only
prize?

'I can't believe you said that,' she declared at last, willing her brain to find a more salutary retort. 'I'm sorry
you're frustrated, Neil. It must be annoying for you. I wonder...?' An answer trembled on her lips, and she wondered
if she dared voice it. 'How long have you been—impotent?'

CHAPTER NINE

IT HAD been unforgivable—and she knew it.

Lying awake the next morning after another restless night, Maggie reviewed that final exchange with Neil with some misgivings. Yet, she argued silently, he had said some unforgivable things to her too. He'd surely deserved her retaliation. She grimaced. He deserved everything he got.

She hadn't waited to see how that crippling enquiry had been received. Before the words had left her mouth, she had been on her way to the door, and although she had expected him to come after her, expected every second for him to grab her on the stairs, she had reached her room in safety. Of course, she thought now, he wouldn't have wanted to disturb Lindsey. He wouldn't have wanted her to see her father and mother fighting, however subtle the weapons might be. He wanted her to think they were civilised human beings. But, the way he'd made her feel the night before, Maggie felt as if she could have done murder.

Realising that the longer she lay there brooding about it, the harder it was going to be to face her ex-husband again, Maggie swung her legs out of bed. She had to remember she was here for Lindsey, and no one else. If Neil chose to use her as a sparring partner, then it was up to her to prove she was just as able to punch back.

At least she had brought some suitable clothes with her, she thought, shivering as she left the shower. Warm jeans, a chunky sweater and woollen socks inside a pair of Doc Martens more than made up for the lowering of the temperature. A glance outside had shown there had been a hard frost, and last night's sleet lay like a lacy shawl over the frozen earth.

By the time she had dried her hair and put on some make-up, it was after eight o'clock. It was only as she was leaving her room that she realised she didn't know where Lindsey's room was. Had they still been at the dower house, she'd have had no problem in locating her daughter. But Haversham House was a much different proposition, with many doors opening off its long corridors.

As there was little point in trying to find her, Maggie went straight downstairs. She hoped Luke would come to join them for breakfast. It would be easier talking to him than fencing with either Neil or Lindsey.

The fire was burning merrily in the hall grate, but there was no one about. Venturing into the morning room, she found it was deserted too, although it was obvious from the table that someone had already been served. A jug of coffee was cooling beside a half-empty rack of toast, and a rolled-up napkin had been tossed down beside a barely touched plate of scrambled eggs.

Neil?

Maggie glanced apprehensively about her, wondering if whoever had been having breakfast was finished, or had simply been called away. She leant across the table and laid her fingers against the side of the coffee-pot, only to find it was barely lukewarm. Which meant its recipient was long gone.

She bit her lip, wondering if she ought to wait until Lindsey appeared. But, knowing her daughter as she did, it could be eleven o'clock or later before she got out of bed, and even Luke's invitation to go riding was hardly likely to change that.

She was considering pressing the bell to summon Mrs Fenwick when that lady came bustling into the room behind her. 'Why, Ms Freeman!' she exclaimed. 'You should have let me know you were waiting. We've had a bit of an upset in the kitchen, or I'd have had these plates cleared away before now.'

Maggie shook her head. 'I've just come down,' she assured her. And then she asked, 'What kind of an upset?'

'Oh, it was something and nothing,' declared the housekeeper, gathering the used china onto a tray. 'Lindsey spilt a pint of milk over the cat, and the poor thing's been leading us all a dance, trying to get her clean.'

Maggie blinked. 'Lindsey?' She couldn't believe it. Lindsey up before eight o'clock!

'Mmm.' Mrs Fenwick pulled a rueful face. 'Accidents will happen. She and Mr Jordan have gone out now, and she's barely touched her breakfast.'

Maggie stared. 'Those were Lindsey's scrambled eggs?'

'Yes.' Mrs Fenwick brushed the crumbs from the white damask cloth into her hand. 'So, what would you like, Ms Freeman? A mixed grill, or some scrambled eggs as well?'

Maggie swallowed. 'Um—just toast,' she said, when she had gathered herself. She licked her lips. 'Doesn't—Mr Jordan eat breakfast?'

'Bless you, yes,' said Mrs Fenwick. 'But he had a bacon sandwich in the kitchen. While we were trying to catch Tuppence,' she added, with a grimace. 'That poor animal; you should have seen it. It's never been so shocked in its life.'

Maggie bit her lip. 'Is it all right?'

'He is now,' agreed Mrs Fenwick ruefully. 'Mr Jordan dumped him in the sink in the garden room, and made sure he was thoroughly clean. He's drying himself now, in front of the fire. Tuppence, I mean.' She smiled. 'Are you sure you just want toast? You wouldn't like a nice boiled egg?'

'No, thanks.'

As Mrs Fenwick went to get the toast and some fresh coffee, Maggie wandered over to the windows. Perching on the window-seat, she looked out on the garden at the side of the house, where frost-laden trees and hedges made a tracery against the green fields beyond. There were cows in the field that was farthest away from the house, huge, shaggy-coated creatures that she guessed were Highland in origin. But the paddocks nearest the house were empty. It was too cold to leave horses out all night.

She couldn't fault the position of the house. Situated on a rise, it had a wonderful view of the moors and hills that surrounded it. At this time of the year, Northumberland possessed a strange, austere beauty. Something Maggie had never noticed before, she acknowledged. In the past, she'd been too keen to get away.

Which she should be now, she told herself impatiently. After last night, she should have no doubt of Neil's opinion of her. Time had passed, it was true, but in his case it had not made her defection any less unforgivable. His heart hadn't grown fonder. Where she was concerned, it was as unforgiving as stone.

Despite her unease, Maggie managed to eat two half slices of toast, and drink three cups of the strong, aromatic coffee. In fact, were it not for the apprehension she felt every time Mrs Fenwick came into the room, she would have had to admit she was enjoying the sensation of freedom. Most mornings, she swallowed her coffee while she was issuing Mrs Lewis instructions for the day, and it was months since she had troubled to have anything to eat.

And it was not Mrs Fenwick who disturbed her, of course. It was the anticipation of Neil coming into the room and finding her alone. But he had gone out with Lindsey, she assured herself. And Luke must have joined them because he didn't show up either.

With the meal over, Maggie thanked the housekeeper before wandering into the drawing room. This morning, although the fire here had been relaid, it had not been re-lighted, though the room was sufficiently warm from the radiators that lined the walls. She had not realised they were radiators until this moment. Concealed by intricately carved screens, the modern heaters were cleverly hidden from view.

Maggie sighed. She wasn't interested in the pile of news-papers she had seen in the morning room, and staring out of the drawing-room windows all morning didn't have much appeal. She supposed she could go and find Mrs Fenwick in the kitchen, and talk to her, but she didn't want Neil to think she was prying by asking his housekeeper a lot of questions.

So what could she do? she wondered. Put on her outdoor clothes and go looking for the others? No. She'd never shown any interest in horses before, and once again she had no wish to arouse Neil's derision. Perhaps the house had a library. Perhaps she could find herself a book.

It wasn't an appealing notion, but it seemed like the only one she had. Unless she swallowed her pride and went for a walk by herself. Surely even Neil couldn't criticise her for that?

Hurrying upstairs again, she gathered up her overcoat and scarf, and her leather gloves, which were the only ones she had brought with her. They weren't warm, but they were serviceable, and at least they'd stop her hands from getting chapped. Then, slinging the coat about her shoulders, she ran back downstairs.

She doubted whether Lindsey and her father had used the front door to leave the house, but she had no option. Short of telling Mrs Fenwick what she planned to do, of course, and she preferred to keep her activities to herself.

Outside, the wind-chill factor knocked off at least another ten degrees, and Maggie shivered in spite of herself. But the air was crisp and clean and exhilarating, and not choked with exhaust fumes as it was in London.

Deciding to avoid the outbuildings, which were visible at the back of the house, Maggie struck out along a path that ran around the side of the building, before descending through a belt of conifers into a terraced garden. Box-hedges fenced rose and flower gardens, the lawns between trimmed to an admirable neatness, considering the season. Another fountain, like the one at the front of the house, spilled a frosted stream down the hillside which disappeared into a reed-edged pool that was almost concealed by snow.

Dangerous, she thought, touching the frozen rim of the pool with the toe of her boot. An unwary foot could plunge into the water, which was surely cold enough to freeze the blood.

Below the formal gardens, a copse of trees formed a natural barrier to the fields beyond. Underfoot, the leaves from oak and ash made a mulch of the path, and water dripping from the bare branches made an eerie sound.

A glance at her watch informed her that it was barely half-past ten. Far too soon to go back, she decided firmly, even as she hunched her shoulders against the cold. There was a clutch of cottages across the fields; perhaps it was the village. There might even be a café where she could get a hot drink.

An examination of the change in her pocket assured her that she had enough to pay for a cup of tea or coffee, and, hitching up her coat, she made an ungainly traverse of the hedge. Oh, well, she thought as she slipped and went down onto one knee and felt a seeping of dampness through the denim, she'd survive. Whatever Neil thought, she wasn't afraid of the country. In fact, the more she saw of this place, the more she realised how much she had misjudged it before.

Or maybe it was herself she had misjudged, she reflected, remembering how certain she had been that she wanted a life of her own. Had she been jealous of Neil's success? Had she let Jackie persuade her that it was what she wanted? Or was the truth somewhat less discernible? Her life hadn't been about choices; it had been about circumstances she hadn't been able to control.

The ground she was walking on was hard, and rutted from the farmer's efforts with a tractor. It made her progress considerably slower, and she had to take care not to twist her ankle. She could imagine how humiliating that would be—struggling back to Haversham with her ankle swollen to twice its normal size.

She noticed the house before she reached the village, which was proving to be rather farther than she'd originally anticipated. Distances across farmland could be notoriously misleading, she realised, and, glancing round, she was alarmed to find that, despite the fact that Neil's house stood on a rise, it, too, seemed much farther away than she'd thought.

She frowned, tempted to turn back and abandon her plan to reach the village. It was probably just a cluster of cottages anyway, she decided, realising that despite her exertions she was still feeling the cold.

The drone of a vehicle startled her. She had thought she was alone in this wintry landscape of frost-dusted fields and skeletal trees, and the sudden appearance of a Land Rover was unexpected. It accelerated towards her, taking a circuitous route that hugged the hedgerows, and then jolted to a halt a few feet away.

A man swung down from behind the wheel and approached her. He was a broad man, wearing a waxed jacket, and the ubiquitous green boots Maggie had always ridiculed in the past, and his weathered features were creased into a smile. 'It's Maggie, isn't it?' he said, holding out his hand towards her. 'Nic said you were here. It's good to see you again.'

Maggie blinked. 'Do I know you?' She shook her head. 'I'm sorry. You've got me at a disadvantage.'

'Ben Armstrong,' he said, his calloused palm warm even through her glove. His smile was warm, too. 'I haven't changed that much, have I?'

Maggie stared at him. 'You're—Nicola's father!'

'That's right.' Ben Armstrong didn't seem at all put out that she had taken so long to recognise him. 'How are you?'

'I'm—fine.'

It was the stock answer, but Maggie was just so surprised that he should have taken the trouble to speak to her. It was true, they had met before, but it was over five years since she had seen him. In any case, any contact they had had had been limited to social occasions, when Nicola had been angling for Neil's attention.

Besides, Mrs Armstrong had always made sure that he didn't do anything to baulk his daughter's ambitions, such as getting too friendly with Neil's wife. Which made his conduct now that much more unexpected, and she didn't quite know how to deal with his familiarity.

'It's a cold morning to be out on your own,' he said, glancing up at the grey sky. 'I think we're going to have some more snow.'

'Do you?' Maggie followed his example, grimacing at the low-hanging clouds. 'Well, not before I get back, I hope,' she said, pressing her hands together. 'Um—it's been nice seeing you again, Mr Armstrong.'

'Ben,' he corrected her firmly, and gestured back at the Land Rover. 'Let me give you a lift. I'll feel happier knowing you've got home safely. People have been known to lose their way when the conditions are bad.'

'Oh, really—'

'You might even be kind enough to come back to the house for some coffee,' he added, his brows arching hopefully. 'Dare I say I'd welcome the company?'

Maggie didn't know what to say. 'But won't your wife—?'

'My wife died—oh, it must be nearly three years ago now,' he replied without emotion. 'I live alone these days—except for my housekeeper, of course. And Nic makes sure I'm never lonely.' He grimaced. 'At least she does when she can find the time.'

Maggie hesitated. She could insist on going back to Haversham. She had no doubt that if she refused his invitation he'd still give her a lift home. He was that kind of man. But did she really want to go straight back, and maybe run the risk of bumping into his daughter? For she suspected Nicola would be around, particularly as Neil had evidently told her she and Lindsey were staying at the house.

'Well, if you're sure...' she ventured, and Ben Armstrong gave her a beaming smile.

'It'll be my pleasure,' he assured her firmly. 'Come along. Let me help you into the Rover.'

The Armstrongs' house was smaller than Neil's, but it was elegant nonetheless. Originally built in the late nineteenth century, it had been tastefully extended and modernised, so that now it looked less like a farmhouse and more like a small manor house. Dogs came to greet them as the Land Rover pulled into the yard, and Ben Armstrong apologised in advance for their exuberance. 'They're supposed to be guard dogs,' he said as they fussed about the visitor. 'Give them a biscuit and they're anybody's.'

The housekeeper, a dour-faced woman in her fifties, Maggie assumed, gave them coffee in the beamed living room. Whether she remembered her employer's guest from the last time she had come here with Neil Maggie couldn't be certain, but there was no doubt that she resented having to serve her.

Of course, she and Neil had been having problems in those days, Maggie reflected. Not least her own insistence that she couldn't live anywhere but London. How naïve she'd been, she thought ruefully; how sure she'd been of her importance in Neil's life. She'd never dreamt that he might call her bluff, or that her defiance would go so wrong...

Ben Armstrong had helped her to remove her coat, and now he flung off his jacket and seated himself beside her. The leather chesterfield was big enough for Maggie to feel no sense of crowding when he did so, and his attitude was so friendly, she couldn't help but relax.

'So, tell me what you've been doing in recent years,' he invited, after she had accepted one of the shortbread biscuits the housekeeper had so grudgingly supplied. 'I believe Nic said you had opened a shop. A dress shop. Is that right?'

'That's right.' Maggie nibbled on the biscuit, wondering if this was the most sensible thing she had ever done. What if Nicola had asked her father to find out about her? What if this was her idea, not his? 'It keeps me busy.'

'I expect it does.' Ben Armstrong stretched out his legs— broad legs, Maggie noticed—clad in thick brown cords that were thrust into his boots. Viewing him objectively, she guessed he was in his fifties too. Perhaps the housekeeper saw her as a possible rival. If it wasn't so sad, it would be ridiculous.

'Nic—' Maggie cleared her throat. 'Nicola doesn't live at home, then?'

'Oh, no.' Ben Armstrong gave a rueful grimace. 'She offered to come back—when her mother died, you know. But I said, If you're not happy with Jack, you'll have to find somewhere else.'

'Jack—was her husband?'

'Ex-husband,' agreed Ben, pushing back his mop of grey-streaked auburn curls. 'Jack Braithwaite. From Hexham. His family used to farm over there. He was a nice chap. Too nice for our Nicola,' he added, with a chuckle. 'Nic never saw herself as just a farmer's wife.'

Maggie absorbed what he had said. It seemed obvious

that, far from probing into her affairs on Nicola's behalf, Ben Armstrong was cheerfully cynical about his daughter. Maggie realised that if Nicola resembled anyone it must be her mother, a woman who had treated Maggie with a certain amount of contempt.

Conversation became general, and although they barely touched on personal matters Maggie felt at ease in his company. Perhaps that was why, she thought. She didn't feel as if he had any axe to grind. They had come together as equals, and despite the difference in their ages she thought he was an extremely likeable man.

She was almost sorry when it was time for her to go back to Haversham, and she sensed he felt the same. Which was why, when he mentioned how nice it would be to see her again, she didn't immediately say no. Why not? she thought. Neil could hardly object. He'd made his opinion of her far too obvious for her to have any doubts.

It had started to snow while they were having coffee, and Maggie was surprised to see several cars on the forecourt when Ben delivered her back to Haversham House. There was Neil's Range Rover, a Land Rover and several other vehicles, and Ben's brows descended in some surprise.

'I wonder what's going on?' he said, bringing the Land Rover to a halt. ''That's Harry Fitzgerald's Land Rover, and Tom Archer's Toyota. I wonder what they're doing here? I'd have thought they'd have had too much to do, with the weather closing in.'

Maggie frowned as she got out of the vehicle. 'Why?' she asked. 'Who are they?'

'Well, some of these cars belong to Neil's estate workers,' said Ben, 'but Harry and Tom are farmers farther up the valley. It looks like something's happened. Maybe someone's gone missing.'

Lindsey.

Maggie's heart turned over. 'My daughter went out with Neil earlier!' she exclaimed. 'Oh, Ben, you don't think there's been an accident, do you?'

'Not with all these cars here,' said Ben reassuringly. 'At least there isn't an ambulance among them. No. Maybe

Neil's having some kind of meeting. I'm just surprised he didn't mention it to me.'

Maggie's knees felt weak. 'Well, thanks for bringing me home—' she was beginning, when the door of the house opened and Neil himself appeared. At least he was all right, she thought, amazed at how relieved that made her feel, and, raising a hand to Ben, she rushed across the paved courtyard to meet him.

'Maggie!'

His astonishment at seeing her was evident, and she wondered if he had been ringing the Armstrongs' house, trying to reach her. But then she realised he hadn't known she was there. And in any case the phone hadn't rung while they were having coffee.

'Is something wrong?' she cried, aware of Ben getting out of the Land Rover behind her. 'Where's Lindsey? Has something happened to her?'

'Not as far as I know. She's indoors,' said Neil, with a definite edge to his voice. He came down the steps, his expression hardening. 'More to the point, where the hell have you been?'

Maggie swallowed. 'Me?'

'Yes, you.' Neil was obviously finding it hard to keep his temper. 'For God's sake, Maggie, I've been nearly out of my mind with worry. You went out more than two hours ago, and they're forecasting that this—' he gestured to the snow '—is likely to turn into a blizzard.'

'Oh.'

Maggie didn't know what to say in her own defence, and as if realising he should have some input here Ben came forward. 'She's been with me, Neil,' he said ruefully. 'I'm afraid I persuaded her to join me for coffee. I had no idea you'd be worried about her or I'd have called.'

A muscle jerked in Neil's jaw. 'She's been with you?' he echoed harshly. His face darkened. 'I didn't even know you were acquainted.'

'Well, of course we're acquainted!' exclaimed Ben, clearly not enjoying having to explain himself. 'We met— when—when Maggie was living here,' he finished unhappily.

Neil's mouth tightened. 'And you'd never forgotten what she looked like,' he remarked, his tone dangerous. 'How amazing!'

'It wasn't like that,' said Maggie quickly, seeing how their exchange was deteriorating, and desperate to avoid a scene. 'I was—out walking. I'd gone farther than I'd realised, and I was on the point of turning back when Ben found me.'

'Really?' Neil didn't sound as if her explanation cut any ice with him. 'And since when have you taken up fell-walking? I'd have thought a chair in front of the fire was more your bag—'

'I say...' Ben broke in again. 'There's no need to snap, Jordan. If you want my advice, you'll let your—your—Maggie go indoors. She must be frozen. I know I am, standing out here.'

'But I don't want your advice,' said Neil, apparently beyond the bounds of being polite. 'You had no right to interfere; no right to disappear with my wife for hours on end, without telling anyone where she was. I've had a search party out looking for her for the past hour.' He scowled at Maggie. 'We found your footprint by the pond. For an awful couple of minutes, we thought you'd fallen in.'

Maggie sighed. 'As if.'

'As if—nothing.' Neil took a calming breath. 'This isn't Knightsbridge, Maggie. There aren't any convenient taxi ranks around here.'

'I know that.' Maggie was beginning to resent being treated like a disobedient child. 'For God's sake, Neil, all I did was go for a walk. The way you're acting, you'd think I'd been out all night!'

'That's true, Jordan,' put in Ben supportively. 'Your wife's not stupid, old man. It's all been an unfortunate mistake.'

'Yes, it has,' agreed Maggie, grateful to the other man for sticking up for her. 'And I'm not your wife, in case you've forgotten. I don't have to answer to you any more.'

Neil stared at them both for another long, humiliating minute, and then, without another word, he turned and walked back into the house. Maggie suspected, knowing him of old, that he didn't trust himself to say anything else, and with a rueful look up at her companion she turned away.

'I'd better go.' Her coat was turning white, and she had no wish to remind Neil of the weather. She lifted her shoulders. 'Sorry.'

Ben came after her. 'You'll be all right?'

'Oh, of course.' Of that she had no doubt. Neil would regret this scene as soon as he had had time to regain his temper. He'd allowed his emotions to get the better of him, and he wouldn't forgive her for being the cause. 'Thanks again.'

'Can I ring you?'

Ben was endearingly concerned, and Maggie couldn't help putting up her hand and touching his cheek. 'Why not?' she said lightly. 'I may need your support. And, in spite of Neil, I did have a very pleasant morning.'

'I'm glad.'

Ben looked as if he would have liked to return the salutation, but he was evidently conscious of the fact that Neil might be watching them from the house. So, instead, he contented himself with squeezing her hand, before turning and walking back to the vehicle.

The snow was thickening as Maggie started up the steps to the house. Large, fluffy flakes that floated down so gently, it seemed impossible that they should ever weigh down trees and power cables. Impossible, too, that they should ever blanket the ground, she thought incredulously. But already there was a covering at her feet.

Despite her reluctance to see Neil again, it was a relief to get indoors. While she'd been standing on the forecourt, the wind had chilled her thoroughly, and Maggie couldn't wait to do as her ex-husband had so sarcastically remarked and toast her toes before an open fire. This was one occasion when she was glad there were open fires to sit in front of, and she shed her cashmere overcoat and draped it over a chair.

She was warming her hands in front of the burning logs in the hall grate when Neil reappeared. This time, she was prepared for his sarcasm, so it came as something of a disappointment when Lindsey followed him out of a room Maggie had hitherto not entered herself.

'There you are at last, Mum!' she exclaimed, not without an edge of irritation in her voice. 'How many times have you told me not to go out without telling you where I'm going? And then you go swanning off to the Armstrongs' and ruin our morning!'

Maggie stiffened. 'How have I ruined your morning? I thought you were going riding with Luke.'

'Well, I was,' retorted Lindsey ill-temperedly, 'but you had disappeared, hadn't you? Daddy insisted on looking for you, and naturally we were roped in.'

'To do what?'

''What do you think?''

'That will do, Lindsey.'

Both Maggie and Neil spoke at once, and the girl's face took on a sulky expression. Then, turning to his ex-wife, Neil gave an explanation. 'Mrs Fenwick was worried because you appeared to have vanished from the house.'

Maggie caught her breath. 'Oh, this is ridiculous—'

'I agree.' Neil regarded her coldly. 'In future, I'd be grateful if you'd inform someone when you're going out.' His eyes flickered. 'And I can't imagine what you thought you were doing, spending the morning with Ben Armstrong. You hardly know him, for God's sake! Anything could have happened, and we'd have been none the wiser.'

'Oh, honestly.' Maggie stared at him in disbelief. 'You're not going to tell me he's untrustworthy, are you? You're not implying he's the kind of man to—to—well, rape me, or something incredible like that?' She shook her head. 'Might I remind you this is your—' she cast a doubtful glance at Lindsey '—your girlfriend's father? I hardly think she'd appreciate hearing your insinuations.'

Neil's face grew even colder, and Lindsey looked up at her father with some dismay. 'You said she was just a friend, when I asked you,' she complained indignantly. 'Mum's implying that you and she are having an affair.'

'Well, we're not,' said Neil, through his teeth, and

Maggie knew an unwarranted sense of relief. It wasn't that she cared if he had an affair, she assured herself firmly. She was just glad he wasn't having an affair with Nicola.

'Anyway, if you ask me, it was all a fuss over nothing,' went on Lindsey, and Maggie couldn't be sure whether she believed her father or not. 'I told you Mum would be all right, but you wouldn't listen to me.'

'Well, I'm sorry.' Maggie had had enough of this, and, picking up her coat, she started for the stairs. 'I'm going to get changed,' she said, not caring what they thought of her at that moment. 'Oh...' she paused on the fourth stair '...for your information, Ben was a charming host.'

CHAPTER TEN

THE snow was falling heavily now. From her bedroom window, Maggie had an uneasy image of how helpless she would have been, caught out in conditions like these. Trees, hedges, fields—all were being hidden beneath a blanket of white, and landmarks no longer looked familiar as the blizzard thickened.

She sighed. Perhaps she had reacted badly, she thought. Perhaps Neil had only had her best interests at heart, and there was no doubt that if she had been out in the storm she could have got into difficulties. There was no saying where she might have wandered if Ben hadn't found her as he had.

With her boots exchanged for a pair of trainers, and the heavy sweater for a long-sleeved shirt, Maggie sat down at the dressing table to brush her hair. Her reflection looked back at her, unusually flushed and animated, and she realised that, for all her dressing down, she looked healthier than she'd done for years.

When someone knocked at the bedroom door, she didn't hesitate before calling, 'Come in,' and then wished she'd had the sense to ask who it was when her ex-husband came into the room. An inner weariness gripped her. She should have known Neil wouldn't let her get away with the barbed exchange they had indulged in downstairs. He was angry, and he wanted her to know it. But with Lindsey present he hadn't been able to expose his real feelings.

Deciding there was no point in ordering him out again, Maggie did her best to ignore him, continuing to brush her hair as if he weren't standing there, glowering at her in the mirror.

She felt a moment's apprehension when he closed the door behind him, but then decided she would rather no one else knew what was going on. It would only upset Lindsey, and if Mrs Fenwick saw them the gossips would have a field day, particularly as she wasn't absolutely sure what the housekeeper's opinion of her was.

'Are you all right?'

His first words startled her, prepared as she'd been for his censure. Perhaps she was wrong; perhaps he wasn't glowering at her after all. Perhaps what she had seen as anger was really concern.

Some hope!

'Why shouldn't I be?' she responded at once, and then chided herself for the obvious challenge in her voice. If he was prepared to be civil, then she should at least meet him halfway. Hadn't she been sympathising with his reaction just minutes ago?

But it was too late now to wish she had been more conciliatory, and Neil was speaking again. 'I was concerned,' he said. 'Whether you believe it or not. We may not always have been the best of friends, but I wouldn't want anything bad to happen to you.'

'Wouldn't you?' Again, Maggie's tongue was several beats ahead of her brain, and she caught her lower lip between her teeth. 'I'm sorry,' she said, as she had said downstairs, but with rather more sincerity. 'I had no idea you'd be worried.' She put down the brush and turned ruefully to face him. 'I mean it. I thought you and Lindsey would be out all morning.'

'Hmm.' Neil moved away from the door, hands pushed into the back pockets of his tight-fitting jeans, suede waistcoat open over a heavy denim shirt. 'Well, by the time she'd seen the foal and spent a few minutes with each of the other horses, it was beginning to look overcast,' he explained. 'So, instead of going riding, we decided to go for a swim.'

'Oh, I see.'

Maggie wished she could get to her feet without looking as if his standing over her was intimidating her. But, before she could think of a way to extricate herself, Neil lowered

his weight onto the edge of the bed. Which wasn't any
more to her liking, she thought. Sitting there, he looked far
too familiar for her peace of mind.

'Um—Luke too?' she asked, trying to divert herself,
aware that the words came out rather higher than she would
have liked.

'Luke too,' he agreed. 'That was when we wondered if
you would like to join us.' He looked at her steadily. 'Only,
of course, you couldn't be found.'

Maggie lifted her shoulders a little nervously. 'I'm
sorry,' she said again. 'I—just felt like—like a walk.'

'Like getting away, you mean?' suggested Neil, rubbing
the palms of his hands over the taut fabric that covered his
thighs.

'Perhaps,' she conceded softly. 'After last night, I didn't
think you'd want me around.' She paused. 'I suppose I
should apologise. I—didn't mean it.'

'Mean what?' he enquired, equally softly, and she realised he was not as impassive as he appeared.

'You know,' she said unevenly. She cleared her throat.
'Where's Lindsey now?'

'Nursing her grievances in the library, I should think,'
declared Neil drily. 'That's where we were when you got
back. I'd phoned a couple of my neighbours to ask if they'd
seen you, and they insisted on coming over to help us
search the estate. It was always possible you'd fallen, and
weren't able to move.' He shrugged. 'But they've gone
now, thank God!'

Maggie's teeth dug into her lower lip. It was difficult to
be objective when the sight of her ex-husband lounging on
her bed in the middle of the day caused her so much unease.
It was difficult to remember, too, how angry she had been
with him the night before. He was behaving so reasonably
now, yet she still couldn't relax.

'You didn't phone the—the Armstrongs?' she ventured
at last, wondering why Ben Armstrong hadn't been his first
choice. After all, their estates did run side by side for quite
a distance, and in his shoes that was what she'd have done.

'No.' Neil rested back on his elbows now, regarding her
with dark, unreadable eyes. Then, as if realising he owed

her an explanation, he added, with evident reluctance, 'Nic—Nicola said he was going to Carlisle this morning.'

Maggie stiffened. 'You rang Nicola, then?'

'No.' His response was given mildly. 'She told me that last night.' He paused. 'When I rang to tell her I was back from London.'

Maggie pressed her palms together. 'You keep her informed, then? Of your movements, I mean.'

Neil shrugged. 'When it's necessary.'

'And it was necessary last night?' asked Maggie, hearing the accusation in her voice but unable to do anything about it.

'I thought so,' he remarked, without animosity. 'It seemed wisest to warn her that Lindsey was here; that it might not be a good idea to turn up unannounced.'

Maggie's breath felt as if it had been sucked out of her. 'You mean you'd rather Lindsey didn't see you two together, right?' She was scornful. 'In case she got the same impression I did.'

Neil's nostrils flared. 'No.'

'Why, then?'

'I think that's my business, don't you?' With a lithe, impatient movement, he sat upright again. 'Why should it matter to you? It's not as if it has any bearing on what happened between you and me.'

Maggie held his gaze as long as she dared, and then resorted to examining her reflection again. 'No, that's right,' she said crisply. 'How you choose to live your life is your concern. I just find your hypocrisy sickening, that's all.'

'*My* hypocrisy?' he echoed disbelievingly, and despite her efforts to appear calm Maggie could feel herself shaking inside. 'Well, sure,' he added, his voice harshening, 'it's something you're pretty familiar with yourself. Tell me, does Massey deserve his reputation? Is he really as much of a stud as his agency would have us believe?'

Maggie caught her breath, her eyes meeting his in the mirror almost compulsively. 'Why do you want to know?' she asked, refusing to let him see he'd hurt her. 'I can't believe you're still jealous, after all this time.'

It was meant to annoy him, a reckless piece of bravado that was the only way she could think of to eclipse his cruel words. If she'd anticipated any response at all, it was in the form of another crippling denigration, so that when he got up from the bed and came to stand behind her, his hands heavy on her shoulders, she was almost paralysed with shock.

'And if I am?' he asked silkily, massaging the fine bones with strong fingers. 'What then?'

Maggie's breathing was shallow. It was a game, she thought. He hadn't succeeded in belittling her one way, so he was planning to do it another. But what other? she asked herself unsteadily. And how was she going to handle it? Exactly how strong was her bid for self-preservation?

'This isn't going to work,' she said at last, when he met her determined gaze in the mirror. 'I know you're only making fun of me, and you're not going to make a fool of me again.'

'Oh?' His lids shadowed his dark eyes as he watched her. 'And how am I doing that?' His fingers slid to her throat, caressing the smooth skin with evident satisfaction. 'Like this?' he whispered huskily, bending his head to touch the soft lobe of her ear with his tongue. 'Or like this?' He took the fleshy lobe between his teeth, and bit down hard.

'Stop it!'

Maggie would have got to her feet then, but the hands bearing her down prevented her from getting off the stool. 'Not yet,' he said throatily, enjoying her humiliation. 'I haven't finished.'

His thumbs moving against the sensitive pulse behind her ears were hopelessly erotic. She could have twisted her head away—of course she could, she told herself—but she was waiting, just to see how far he intended to go. After all, she assured herself, it wasn't as if she was participating. If he wanted to play these silly games, then she should use them to her own advantage.

If she could...

'You taste so good,' he said, looking at her through his lashes—long, thick lashes, she noticed unwillingly, shading

eyes that at this moment were as black as ebony. 'I'd forgotten how you tasted,' he went on. 'I've forgotten a lot of
things about you, I guess. You do still use the same perfume. I can smell it on your skin.'

Oh, God!

Maggie's throat was tight. 'Don't,' she said, forgetting
any idea of controlling his demands. Just that one word:
'Don't'. It was all she could get past the constriction that
seemed to be choking her. But, as she'd half expected, Neil
ignored her.

'Your pulse is racing,' he said, moving the collar of her
shirt aside and exposing the pale skin of her shoulder. 'Now
why is that?' he taunted. 'Is it possible you're lying to me
again?'

Maggie gulped. 'I never lied to you.'

'You did, but we won't go into that now,' retorted Neil
smoothly. Watching his hands moving in the mirror, he
loosened the top two buttons of the shirt. 'That's better,
isn't it? I think you must be running a temperature, your
skin's so hot.'

Maggie made an abortive effort to shift from the stool,
but once again his hands held her down. 'Relax,' he said
huskily. 'We've got all the time in the world.' He straddled
the stool beside her, practically imprisoning her between
his knees. 'Now, why don't you let me make love to you?
I promise I won't let you down this time.'

'Neil—'

'That's right.' With one arm securely about her waist, he
began loosening all the buttons on the shirt. 'Just say my
name if it pleases you. I don't mind.'

Maggie took a trembling breath. 'Why are you doing
this?' she cried, hearing the appeal in her voice and de-
spising herself for it. She should never have let him in here.
As soon as she'd realised who it was, she should have ordered him out of her room.

'Don't you like it?' he asked, his eyes darkening at the
sight of the provocative scrap of lace she called a bra. 'I
do,' he went on firmly, and she wondered if she had only
imagined the sudden catch she'd heard in his voice.

She took another breath. 'What if Lindsey comes looking

for us?' she asked—anything to avoid accentuating the intimacy of the moment.

'She won't.' Neil was depressingly certain about that. 'I told her I wanted to talk to you, and that we didn't want to be disturbed.'

Maggie shook her head. 'And since when has Lindsey done what you asked her to do?' she asked unsteadily, and Neil's mouth curved in a mocking smile.

'Since I've got something she wants,' he replied carelessly. 'She still thinks she can make me change my mind.'

'About—about Mike Reynolds?'

Maggie was desperate to keep their conversation away from the disturbing familiarity of his hands, and Neil shrugged. 'What else?' he countered, looking at her reflection in the mirror. His tongue appeared to moisten his upper lip in thoughtful consideration. 'Doesn't your skin look pale against mine?'

'Neil—'

'That's my name,' he agreed, rubbing the pad of his thumb across one lace-covered nipple. 'Oh, you're not cold, are you?' Her skin was feathering helplessly. 'We'll have to do something about that—but not yet.'

Maggie tried to keep calm. She could get out of this—she *would* get out of this—if she could just keep her head. It wasn't as if he hadn't seen her body before; it wasn't as if it was the first time he'd undressed her. She had no secrets from him, for heaven's sake, so why did she feel as if he'd never done this before?

'Oh, Maggie, I do believe you like this,' he said wickedly as her nipple hardened and pressed against the lace. 'Look,' he invited her, but she refused to meet his gaze in the mirror. 'I'd forgotten what a sensual creature you are.'

Maggie ground her teeth together, looking anywhere but at him, and then she was forced to suck in her breath when he bent his head and took her nipple into his mouth. The fine lace was no protection against the probing brush of his tongue, or the playful possession of his teeth.

Her eyes flew to the mirror then, watching his dark head at her breast with horrified fascination. At least he couldn't see her reaction, she thought as he continued his sensual assault. The trouble was, she was affected by it, and she could feel his hot tongue inciting unwelcome waves of need inside her.

When he lifted his head, she was gazing out of the window, as if there was any chance of her finding a solution there. But at least he couldn't be sure that she had been watching him, and his mouth twisted lazily at the sight.

'It's still snowing,' he commented, the covering veil of whiteness giving the room an unnatural glow. 'But it's cosy here, isn't it?' he added, his fingers on her chin, turning her face towards him. 'Come on; tell me you agree with me. You'd rather be here than outside.'

An idea occurred to her. 'Than with Ben Armstrong, you mean?' she demanded, refusing to look at the devastating curl of his mouth. 'Well, actually, no. I wouldn't. He's a gentleman—but I don't suppose you know what that is.'

Neil's expression altered. 'You liked him, did you?' he enquired, but although she searched for some reaction there was little expression in his voice.

'Very much,' she replied, wishing she could pull the two sides of her shirt together. It was ridiculous conducting this kind of conversation when she was half-undressed.

'Mmm.' Whatever advantage she might have gained was evidently lost to her. 'Well, you could be right, although Nic's mother wouldn't have agreed with you. You should have heard what she had to say about him and Eileen Barlow.'

Barlow? Maggie frowned, and her eyes were drawn to Neil's against her will. *Mrs* Barlow; hadn't that been the name of Ben's housekeeper? She couldn't believe it. He wouldn't have had anything to do with any relation of hers.

'I see the name means something to you,' remarked Neil softly, trailing his hand down the hollow between her breasts to the sensitive circle of her navel. 'I dare say you met her yourself this morning. I must say, she's never struck me as being particularly handsome.'

Maggie knocked his hand away. 'You don't mean—'

'That's right. Eileen Barlow's his housekeeper. Has been for years. Which might account for the attraction. She was probably better looking when she was younger.'

'I don't believe you.'

'That's your prerogative, of course.'

But it might account for the woman's animosity, thought Maggie reluctantly. Dear God, she'd never dreamt the woman could be jealous!

'Having second thoughts?' he breathed, ignoring her attempts to push him away and releasing the button at her waist. He unzipped her jeans, and slid his hand inside, cupping the warm mound of her sexuality. 'Oh, Maggie, I think I'm going to have to have you.' He drew an uneven breath. 'Open your legs. I want to find out if you're ready.'

Maggie's nerve snapped. 'No,' she said, hearing the break in her voice, but unable to do anything about it. 'Don't touch me, Neil. I hate you for doing this to me.'

She turned then, catching him unawares, and managing somehow to extricate herself from his provocative hands. With a cry that was half sob, half moan, she tore herself away from him, only to sprawl full-length on the cream carpet when her jeans fell about her ankles and brought her down.

She uttered a defeated groan, and he was beside her in a second, flinging himself down to the floor, cupping her face in his hands and staring down at her with anxious eyes. 'Are you all right?' he demanded, fiercely, glancing swiftly over her. 'Oh, God, I'm sorry. I didn't want you to hurt yourself.'

'Are you saving that pleasure for yourself?' she retorted half-tearfully, the fall, following on from his prolonged emotional offensive, causing a pricking at the back of her eyes.

'No,' he said harshly, lowering his head to brush his lips back and forth over hers. 'Oh, God, Maggie, don't be stupid. You know what I want to do.'

She wanted to resist him. When his mouth eventually settled on hers, she wanted to press her lips tightly together and show him there was no way she was going to give in. But her mood was broken. She no longer had the strength— or the will—to turn her head away, and his tongue slid almost unhindered between her teeth.

The kiss deepened and lengthened. Although she wanted

to close her eyes and submit to the delicious sensations it was arousing inside her, she knew she should keep them open. Not that she needed her sight to know that he was lying half over her, that one muscled thigh was between her legs, abrading the sensitive place between her thighs. Or that his hand was cupping her breast, and the weakness that was flooding her knew no bounds.

She felt his hand slide down, over her midriff and the slight swell of her stomach to the waistband of her panties. As he bit her lower lip, before sucking the tip of her tongue and drawing it into his mouth, she tried to keep a hold on her senses. But it was almost impossible to think sensibly, with his weight practically robbing her of breath, and when he ground his hips against hers and she felt the unmistakable thrust of his arousal she knew her accusation of impotence for the pathetic defence it was.

'I want you,' he said, burying his face in the warm hollow between her breasts. He found the front fastening of her bra, and, releasing it, cradled the two swollen globes in his hands. Then, shifting slightly, he bestowed a burning trail of kisses from her breasts, down across the creamy mound of her stomach, only stopping at her navel, to sensitise it with his seductive tongue.

Maggie was beyond knowing what she wanted any more. Neil had always been able to do this to her—to make such sweet love to her that she couldn't think of anyone but him. In the months following their separation and subsequent divorce, she had ached with her need of him, often waking from fitful sleep to find herself wrapped around his pillow.

But this was no dream, this was real, and her head was swimming with the emotions he could so effortlessly arouse in her. She didn't just want him now, she thought; he had always been a part of her, and tears overspilled her lashes at the memories he evoked.

He was skimming the lace briefs down her legs now, pushing off her shoes and jeans, and freeing her legs so that she was able to wind them about him. She caressed his jean-clad calf with the sole of her foot, and felt his instantaneous reaction, the impatience he was controlling so that he could give her pleasure.

And he was giving her pleasure, a wild sexual pleasure that was instantly focused when he pressed his face against the triangle of hair that hid her femininity. With one hand he spread the curls to find the sensitive nub he sought, and then used his tongue to bring her almost to the brink of total surrender.

'God, Neil,' she choked, when he drew away, half afraid this was another form of torture, but his eager mouth assured her this wasn't so. With a stifled oath when the zip briefly baulked, he tore off his own jeans, and moved between her legs. And just when she thought she couldn't wait a moment longer he filled her with his heat.

It hurt. Just for a moment, it actually hurt when he thrust himself inside her, but then her muscles relaxed and expanded to accommodate his need. No one else had ever filled her as Neil's powerful body filled her, and she wound her arms around his neck and brought his lips to hers.

'God, you're tight,' he groaned against her mouth, but she could tell from the glazed satisfaction in his eyes that he wasn't complaining. Her legs wrapped about him, imprisoning him inside her, and she thought if he moved an inch she wouldn't be able to stop the wild cascade.

But, of course, he did move, slowly at first, hands braced beside her head, so that he wouldn't crush her breath with his superior weight. And then more quickly, so that Maggie spun away on a headlong loop of sensation, climaxing, and then climaxing again, as he took her higher and higher.

His own release came only seconds later. He uttered a hoarse cry, and then she felt the hot spurt of his seed inside her. For what seemed like for ever, he jerked helplessly against her, and then collapsed in a heap on top of her, almost stopping her quivering breath...

CHAPTER ELEVEN

'How long do you think we're going to have to stay here?'

Lindsey was standing at her mother's bedroom window, staring out at the huge snowdrift that had completely blocked the drive. It was three days since the snow had started falling, three days since Neil had seduced her, and changed her life...

'Daddy says the snowploughs haven't been able to clear the main road yet,' Lindsey continued, smoothing her palms over her legging-clad thighs. 'I was watching the news last night, and according to the weather bureau more snow is forecast.'

Only he hadn't seduced her—not really, Maggie concluded ruefully, her train of thought moving along a different track. She could have stopped him, if she'd really wanted to. Only she hadn't...

'Daddy thinks we might be here for another week,' persisted Lindsey, and Maggie sighed and pushed herself up onto her pillows. Her daughter was not going to go away, and it was no use pretending she wasn't awake. She had already eaten the toast and drunk the coffee that Mrs Fenwick had delivered to her, and until Lindsey's arrival she had been contemplating going for a long, leisurely bath.

'Does it worry you?' she enquired now, unable—or unwilling—to answer the question herself. The longer they were here, the longer she could delay thinking about the future, and although that was a cowardly thought—and she knew it—it was the only one she had.

Lindsey shrugged, and turned to look at her mother, propped up in the huge bed. 'Sometimes it does, sometimes it doesn't,' she admitted with rather more honesty than her mother had shown. 'I'm not bored, if that's what you're thinking. As a matter of fact, I never realised how much there was to do about the estate. And I love looking after the horses, even if we haven't been able to have our ride yet.'

Maggie pulled a wry face. 'I suppose I'm to blame for that.'

Lindsey grinned, and Maggie realised it was months since she and her daughter had had such a non-combative conversation. These days, they always seemed to be speaking *at* one another, rather than *with*, but suddenly Lindsey was approachable again. And all because of a few horses. And Neil...

'We'll make it, eventually,' said Lindsey now, sauntering towards the bed. 'At least Tim has cleared the yard. We're going to give the hunters some exercise later on.'

'Tim?'

Maggie hadn't heard that name before, and Lindsey adopted a more defensive stance. 'Tim Fitzgerald,' she said carelessly. 'His father has a sheep farm farther up the valley.'

'I see.' Maggie tried not to sound too interested. 'Does he work for your father, then?'

'No.' Lindsey was scornful. 'He's not much older than I am. He's still at school, working for his A levels. He wants to go to university in the autumn, and train to be a vet.'

'Ah.' Maggie absorbed the information with less enthusiasm. For a moment, she'd thought Lindsey might be interested in this Tim. 'So why isn't he at school?'

Lindsey pulled a face. 'What have we been talking about, Mum?' she exclaimed exasperatedly. 'The weather! The roads are blocked. The schools are closed. Haven't you heard a word I've said?'

'Of course I have.' Maggie sighed, hunching her shoulders under the quilt, which she had drawn up about her ears. 'I suppose I just wasn't thinking.' She moistened her lips. 'Where's your father now?'

'Oh, he's in the library—with Mrs Braithwaite,' admitted Lindsey unwillingly, thereby explaining part of the reason why she was here. 'She came as Daddy and I were having breakfast. I don't think she was expected, but Daddy didn't seem to mind.'

'Oh.' Maggie managed to control her expression, and offered her daughter a small smile. 'So, what did you think? I suppose it's the first time you've seen her since we arrived. What with—what with the weather and all, she hasn't been around as often as usual.'

Lindsey looked at her consideringly. 'How do you know how often she comes around?' she asked. 'Did Daddy tell you?'

'No.' Maggie was wary now. 'It—it was just an impression I got from—from Luke, actually.'

'So Daddy hasn't discussed his plans with you?'

Maggie almost gasped. 'No. Why would he?'

'I just wondered.' Lindsey scuffed the toe of her boot against the carpet. 'You and Daddy seemed to be getting along so well.'

Did they?

Maggie knew a moment's panic. She wondered what her daughter would think if she knew the truth. That, since the morning Neil had come to her room and made love to her, they hadn't had a normal conversation; that Neil was careful to tread warily around her, as if he was afraid she might mention what had happened.

'Anyway, I didn't see much of her,' remarked Lindsey now, evidently assuming her mother was waiting for her to make a comment. 'She seemed all right. A bit arrogant, perhaps. I think she'd like to boss Daddy around.'

Maggie was sure of it. Her own encounter with Neil's girlfriend had left her with a distinct sense of unease. Not just because the woman had been rude to her; that wasn't important. But because she was very much afraid she wouldn't make Neil happy, and after his experience with her he deserved better.

'Well, I'm sure he can handle it,' Maggie observed firmly, determined not to let it worry her, and Lindsey lifted her shoulders in a dismissive gesture.

'I guess,' she agreed offhandedly. Then she said, 'Do

you think she'll be staying long? Daddy said he might join me in the gym later on.'

Maggie drew up her legs and wrapped her arms about her knees. 'I honestly don't know,' she said. 'Why don't you ask him?'

'Because I got the feeling she didn't want me around,' replied Lindsey unhappily. She brightened. 'You wouldn't like to join me instead?'

'In the gym?'

Maggie was taken aback, but Lindsey was enthusiastic. 'Why not?' she exclaimed. 'You haven't even had a swim in the pool yet. Oh, you must need some exercise. All you've done is sit and read or watch television since you got here.'

'Well, as you pointed out earlier, the weather hasn't—'

'I know.' Lindsey didn't wait for her mother to finish before plunging on with her spiel. 'But you're always saying you're not fit, and surely this is the perfect opportunity. At least you can't make the excuse that Aunt Jackie is waiting to see you.'

Maggie pressed her lips together. 'All the same—'

'All the same—what?'

'Well...' Maggie hesitated '...I don't have anything to wear.'

'To do what? To go swimming? There are spare swimsuits in the changing rooms. And as for working out—well, you can borrow something of mine.'

Her mother gave her an old-fashioned look. 'Oh, yes?' She uttered a short, self-derisive laugh. 'I may once have had a figure like yours, Lindsey, but those days are long gone.' She grimaced at her daughter's crestfallen expression. 'Oh, I probably packed some leggings in my case.'

Lindsey's eyes widened. 'You mean you'll do it? You'll come?'

Maggie grimaced again. 'I'm not promising to stay long.'

'But you'll do it,' said Lindsey delightedly. 'Well, hurry up. I suppose you'll want to clean your teeth first?'

'I had intended to have a bath,' remarked Maggie regretfully, sliding her legs out of bed. 'But I suppose I can

have that later. I may need it. I am hopelessly out of con-
dition.'

Three-quarters of an hour later, dressed in navy blue leggings and a matching cotton vest, her hair dragged into a
stubby ponytail with an elastic band, Maggie lay back on
the bench press, her arms aching from the unfamiliar stress
of lifting weights. Her thighs ached too, from using the leg
curl, and every inch of her body felt as if it was bathed in
sweat.

Beside her, Lindsey tramped merrily away on the
climber, her forehead slightly dampened, but showing no
other signs of distress. Maggie guessed her face was as red
as a tomato, and even her hair felt as if it was clinging to
her scalp.

'Had enough?' asked Lindsey lightly, looking down at
her mother's flushed face with some concern. 'Don't
overdo it, now. You know what they say: little and often.
At least to begin with, anyway. That's what Daddy told
me.'

'Did he?' said Maggie cynically, wondering if the muscles in her arms would ever stop shaking. 'And, yes, I've
had enough. I think I'll go and have my bath.'

'Oh, not yet.' Lindsey climbed off the machine she had
been using and stood with her hands on her hips, studying
her mother with critical eyes. 'A shower first, to freshen
you up, and then a swim in the pool. Believe me, that's the
best way to recover. We can skip the sauna for today.'

'Gee, thanks.' Maggie struggled into an upright position,
and ran a weary hand around the back of her neck. 'But I
don't know about going swimming, Lindsey.' Even the
thought of putting on a swimsuit made her feel self-
conscious.

'But you must,' Lindsey was saying as the door to the
gym opened and, to Maggie's dismay, Neil and Nicola
Braithwaite appeared in the aperture. The girl swore softly,
and Maggie hadn't the heart to reprove her. It was a sen-
timent she endorsed entirely.

'So, here you are,' said Neil shortly, his gaze flicking
over Maggie's rounded shoulders before coming to rest on

his daughter. 'I—we've been looking for you, Lindsey. You disappeared as soon as Nic arrived.'

'I didn't want to intrude,' said Lindsey, facing her father defensively. 'And Mum was keen to try the equipment, so I thought it was a good time to do it.' She gave her mother an entreating look, begging her to back her up. 'Um—we were just going for a swim, weren't we?'

Maggie knew there was nothing for it but to get to her feet, though she did so rather more slowly than usual. The trouble was, her legs were like jellies—which matched the rest of her, she thought ruefully. This was one occasion when she would have wished to be as thin as Nicola.

'Yes, we were,' she agreed, even though the decision had been in some doubt earlier. She managed a tight smile. 'How nice to see you again, Nicola. Obviously the snow hasn't deterred you.'

Nicola gave Neil a proprietorial look. 'Oh, you know how it is. Neil keeps delivering such cryptic messages. He tells me not to worry about him, but he secretly hopes I will.'

'Really?' Maggie exchanged a look with her ex-husband that could in no way be misconstrued. 'So you came racing through the snow to rescue him from the clutches of his ex-wife and daughter?'

'Well, hardly that,' answered Nicola hurriedly, clearly not wanting to alienate Lindsey. 'But it is almost a week since we've seen one another. You understand, don't you, Maggie? I'm sure there's some man in London you're longing to see.'

'Mum doesn't go out with men,' declared Lindsey, with unexpected vehemence. 'When Daddy walked out, she had to make do with me.'

'Really?' Nicola didn't like being contradicted. 'Well, that's not the way I heard it.'

'I don't think anyone's interested in something that happened over five years ago,' put in Neil, his eyes glinting. 'Do you want to join us at the stables, Lindsey? I think it's time we let Midnight smell some fresh air.'

'Oh—' Lindsey started to say something, and then seemed to think better of it. 'I—no.' Then again, 'No,' she

answered stiffly. 'As I said before, Mum and I were just
going for a swim.'

Neil's jaw hardened. 'That's not going to take all morning.'

'It might.' Maggie knew of old how stubborn Lindsey
could be when she chose. 'You go ahead, Daddy. I'm sure
Mrs Braithwaite will keep you company. After all, that's
why you've been phoning her, isn't it?'

'I haven't—' Neil, too, started to make some retort, and
then clamped his mouth shut on the words. 'Look—' he
took a breath '—this is obviously not a good time to discuss
anything. Your mother looks hot. I think you should both
take a shower before you catch a chill.'

'Don't patronise me, Neil.'

Maggie was in no mood to take that from her ex-
husband. He had had no right to bring Nicola in here without first ascertaining whether they would object. She wondered what was going through his mind as he stood there,
glowering at her. Certainly not the weakness he had allowed to get the better of him three days ago.

What was he thinking as his lips tightened into a thin
line and a look of raw frustration crossed his face? He resented her comment, that went without saying, but what
other thoughts was he harbouring as he fought a losing
battle with his patience?

He must be aware of the fact that their relationship had
suffered since the time he'd come to her room. Whatever
motive he had had in coming to see her, she was sure he
had had no intention of letting things go as far as they had.
He'd been as shocked as she by the unwelcome passion in
their embrace, and he must deeply regret his involvement,
which had blossomed into sexual need.

Yet, at first, when Neil had found his own release and
rolled away from her, pain and disillusionment had not
been her most pressing emotions. What they had shared had
seemed too rich, too deep, too instinctive to run away from.
Whatever Neil had intended when he'd begun tormenting
her in front of the mirror, it had lost its sting. In her arms,
he'd been obsessed, and totally out of control...

'You mistake common concern for some other emotion

best known to yourself,' Neil declared now, tamping down his anger. He turned back towards the door, his hand at Nicola's elbow. 'We'll be in the stables if anyone wants us.'

The atmosphere was still tense even after their departure and Maggie looked at her daughter with troubled eyes. Although Lindsey knew nothing of the scene that had taken place after her mother's return from the Armstrongs', it was too much to hope that she wouldn't want some answers now.

Dear God, she wanted some answers, thought Maggie, though hers, she realized, could only be given by herself. What had she been thinking when Neil had rolled away from her? What had she expected him to say?

In the event, he had said very little beyond a cursory word of apology as he'd got to his feet. Maggie had been left in the ignominious position of having to reach for her shirt to cover herself as her ex-husband pulled on his jeans and tucked in his shirt.

He had made one comment before he went out of the door, she remembered, but she'd taken that as she'd taken so much else. His, 'We have to talk,' had been just a polite way of getting out of a difficult situation, and since then there'd been no opportunity made to make good on his words.

Now, looking at Lindsey, she saw her speculation. Despite her automatic defence of her mother, the girl was bound to be wondering exactly what Nicola had meant. Her remarks had posed an obvious question, and she didn't have to wait long before her daughter spoke.

'What did that woman mean by implying you slept around?' Lindsey demanded fiercely. 'What lies has Daddy been telling her? It was his fault he walked out.' She hesitated. 'Wasn't it?'

Maggie had been afraid this day might come ever since she'd learned that Nicola was back in Neil's life. It was useless now to regret how, years ago, she had begged Neil not to tell their daughter why they were splitting up. She'd persuaded him—and he'd agreed—for Lindsey's sake, she knew—not to sully their daughter's ears with all the sordid details. So far as Lindsey was concerned, their separation had been a mutual arrangement, and the divorce that had followed had been unopposed.

"Your father did choose to walk out," Maggie conceded now, bending to pick up the sweatshirt she had worn to come down to the gym. Dear God, she thought grimly, what was this going to do to Lindsey? It would have been easier telling a ten-year-old, after all.

Lindsey frowned. 'So why didn't you say something?' she exclaimed. 'Why did you let that woman insinuate that you were something you're not?' She blew out another breath in obvious frustration. 'I don't know what Daddy sees in her. It's not as if she's particularly glamorous or anything.'

Maggie sighed, and straightened. 'What if I told you that she had some basis for her accusations?' She watched her daughter closely. 'What then?'

Lindsey blinked. 'You're not going to tell me you did sleep around, are you?' She blew out another breath. 'I don't believe you.'

Maggie took a moment to pull the sweatshirt over her head. 'Your confidence is heartening,' she said ruefully, pulling the fleecy cotton down around her hips. 'But perhaps you should ask your father what happened, not me.'

Lindsey frowned. 'I don't have to.'

Maggie drew an uneven breath. 'Thanks.'

'So...' Lindsey was evidently groping for words. 'Why did you say she has some basis for her accusations?' She paused. 'What really happened?'

Maggie shook her head. 'Ask your father.'

'I'm asking you.' Lindsey came round the exercise bench until they were standing next to one another. 'Come on, Mum. I'm listening. I want to know the truth.'

Maggie wet her dry lips. 'I honestly don't think I'm the one to tell you,' she said, crossing her arms at her waist, as if by doing so she could contain the panic in her stomach. 'I'm afraid I'm biased. If you have to hear the story, I'd rather you heard it from him.'

Lindsey sighed. 'Why shouldn't I believe you? You've never lied to me before.'

'Because—' Maggie could hear the break in her voice and despised herself for it. For God's sake, it was no use regretting the past now. It was over, and the consequences wouldn't change. 'Because there was—another man.'

'Well, I'd rather gathered that,' said Lindsey, with unexpected dryness. 'But I'd still like to know why it happened.' She hesitated, and Maggie could see a certain anxiety in her face. 'Was it—was it Daddy? Had your relationship—well, lost its appeal?'

'No!' Maggie wouldn't have her thinking that, no matter how stupid it sounded now. 'All right. I'll try and explain what happened. From my point of view, I mean. How your father chooses to interpret it is something else.'

'Were you in love with him?'

'Who? Your father?'

'No. This other man,' said Lindsey impatiently. 'I'm just trying to understand what the attraction was, if you and Daddy were still together.'

Maggie sighed, and, realising her legs were in danger of giving out on her, for more reasons than one, she quickly squatted down on the end of the bench. 'No, I wasn't in love with him,' she averred, wishing it didn't sound so pathetic. 'I suppose I'd better begin at the beginning. Explain the reasons why Jackie and I decided to open the first shop.'

'Aunt Jackie knew him, then?'

'What?' Maggie was momentarily diverted by her daughter's question, but then, realising that Lindsey was trying to get the details straight in her own mind, she nodded. 'Oh, yes,' she said. 'Jackie knew him too.'

'So, go on.'

'Well…' Maggie glanced up at her daughter, wishing she didn't feel like such a fraud. This wasn't the way she had hoped to spend the morning, and by alienating Lindsey still further she was only playing into Neil's hands. 'When I first married your father, I was still modelling. But Neil was touring a lot in those days, and he wanted me to go with him.' She pulled a wry face. 'What am I saying? I wanted to go with him. He toured all over the world, and it was an incredible experience for both of us.'

'So you gave up modelling?'

'You know I did.' Maggie grimaced. 'You were born just a few months later.' She shook her head. 'I didn't appreciate just how lucky I was.'

'What happened?'

'Oh, nothing at first.' Maggie was thoughtful. 'We came back to England for a while, and lived in Buckinghamshire, as you know. You started school then, and I got involved in car pools and Brownies. I still used to travel with your father, when I could, and we got a nanny for you.'

'I remember.'

Lindsey nodded, and Maggie moistened her lips before going on. 'I suppose things came to a head when Aunt Jackie was going through her divorce. Your father had never liked her much, as you know. His sympathies were all with Uncle David. Which made it rather difficult when Jackie came to the house, particularly as she was so unhappy at that time. I was in the middle, trying not to let either of them influence me, and having my own small crisis of identity as well.'

Lindsey frowned. 'A crisis of identity?'

'Oh...' Maggie sighed. 'It seems so petty now. I've come to the conclusion I must have been envious of your father's success, and resented the fact that I'd had to give up my career. In any event, I thought I wanted more out of life than just being a wife and mother, and your father naturally found it hard to understand my feelings.'

Lindsey bit her lip. 'And what did Aunt Jackie say?'

'She backed me up, naturally. Jackie has always been absurdly loyal. I suppose with Mum and Dad getting killed in that car crash just after you were born we are much closer than we might have been. And I was foolish enough to think that if Neil could be a success so could I.'

Lindsey looked sympathetic. 'But you couldn't.'

'No.' Maggie sighed again. 'And it was around that time that your father was having trouble with—with his career too.' She was loath to mention Mike Reynolds so she avoided it. She filled her lungs with air. 'He—he decided he'd had enough of making records, and that he wanted to become a full-time composer. He wanted to go back to his roots, which is why he bought the house here, in Northumberland.'

Lindsey appeared to be absorbing every word she said, but Maggie guessed she was impatient for her to get to the point of her story. So far, Maggie had told her little she didn't already know, and she was afraid she'd think that her mother was chickening out.

'Of course I didn't want to live up here,' she continued cautiously. 'I wanted my own life—and a career in London. Although your father had already bought the dower house, I was convinced I could make him change his mind. I thought, if I insisted on staying in the south—and maybe proving I was independent—he'd see it was the only thing to do.'

'But he didn't.'

'Unfortunately not.'

'So...'

'So Jackie and I opened the first Frock Shop, and I stayed on my own.'

Lindsey looked thoughtful. 'Did you have an affair?'

'No.' Maggie tugged the elastic band from her hair and shook the damp, silky strands loose about her shoulders. 'But I did go to parties, and I guess I did try to make your father jealous. But I didn't sleep around, no matter what anyone says.'

'Then what—?'

'There was this man,' said Maggie hurriedly. 'His name was—is—Oliver Massey—'

'The actor?'

Maggie pulled a wry face. 'That's right. He's become more of a household name with working in television. When I knew him, he was mainly known for his work in the theatre.'

'Cool!'

Lindsey whistled, and Maggie felt a ridiculous desire to laugh. But it wasn't because she found what she was doing funny. It was just the fact that her daughter was so impressed.

'He was popular,' she allowed now, remembering how flattered she had been when he'd shown he was attracted to her. 'And he was younger then, and he seemed to enjoy my company.'

'So you slept with him.'

Maggie groaned. 'It wasn't that simple.'

'Then how was it?'

Maggie bent her head, pushing her hands into the pockets of her sweatshirt. Now for the crunch, she thought, dreading the moment. If Lindsey didn't believe her, she'd want to die.

'Well, your father was living up here, as I said before,' she began evenly. 'He hadn't yet decided to sell the house in Buckinghamshire, so I was still living there. But I spent most of my time in London—opening the shop, getting to know the wholesalers, going to shows; there was plenty to do.'

'And you started seeing Oliver Massey?'

'Occasionally. Though in my own defence I have to say that he always seemed to be wherever I went. Actors are always welcome at these shows. The publicity is good for business. And Oliver was so charming, he was invited everywhere.'

'And where was I, while you were inventing your career?'

Maggie shrugged. 'With me. Except in the school holidays, of course. Your father made sure you spent all your holidays with him.' She chanced another look. 'You've always been very close to your father.'

'I've always been very close to both of you,' amended Lindsey firmly, giving Maggie some hope. 'I just wanted you to stay together. I didn't know how much until—well, until recently.'

That was a thought for Maggie to ponder, but she couldn't deal with it at present. 'I know,' she said. 'I realise now I never tried to understand your father's reasons for wanting to move away from London. I seem to have made a mess of all our lives.'

'You shouldn't blame yourself.' Lindsey was unexpectedly defensive. 'I don't suppose Daddy was very supportive when you wanted to open the shop.'

'Well, he never tried to stop me,' said Maggie honestly.

'And without his financial assistance I'd never have had the money to do it.'

'Oh, well…' Lindsey shrugged. 'That's not important now, is it? Perhaps if you'd both tried to understand one another's position it would never have come to a divorce.'

Out of the mouths of babes and sucklings, thought Maggie ruefully, gazing at her daughter with admiring eyes. Perhaps if she and Neil had tried to work it out they wouldn't be in this position. She'd never stopped loving him, no matter how she might deny it to herself.

'I suppose it was because you were on your own that you fell for Oliver Massey,' Lindsey ventured now, and Maggie hastened to put her straight.

'I didn't fall for him,' she said, 'although you may find that hard to believe, I know. What happened wouldn't have happened if I hadn't had too much to drink.'

She expelled a breath, and then continued, 'I told you there were parties, and there were. Almost every night, if that was what you wanted, and after being married for ten years I convinced myself that I deserved some excitement in my life. There was always plenty to drink on those occasions—drugs, too, if you wanted them.' She pulled a face. 'But I was never quite that stupid.'

Lindsey frowned. 'Did Aunt Jackie go with you?'

'Sometimes.' Maggie lifted her shoulders. 'Sometimes, she encouraged me to go on my own.' She grimaced. 'I used to wonder if she hoped I'd get involved with Oliver. She was still smarting over her own divorce, and perhaps she didn't want the same thing to happen to me.'

'But surely she was inviting it?'

'I meant the fact that Uncle David was having an affair. Perhaps she thought Neil wasn't to be trusted either. He was living up here on his own—for most of the time, anyway—and I'd made the mistake of telling her about Nicola.'

Lindsey's brows ascended. 'What about Nicola?'

'Oh, nothing. It was nothing.' The last thing Maggie wanted was for Neil to think she had been filling their daughter's head with ideas. 'Only—' She hesitated. 'Nicola and I were never going to be the best of friends. And I suppose Aunt Jackie put two and two together and made five.'

Lindsey still looked doubtful, but Maggie hurried on. 'Anyway, as I say, Oliver was always around, and I was flattered. The only thing was, I thought I was calling the shots. Then, one night—well, let's just say he got the wrong impression. I'm not going to say he raped me, but he certainly took advantage of me without my consent.'

Lindsey's face was pale. 'Oh, Mum!'

'I know.' Maggie didn't dare to look at her. 'You have no idea how disgusted I was with myself. Unfortunately, I made the mistake of confessing what had happened to your father.' She hunched her shoulders. 'He started divorce proceedings the following week.'

'Citing Oliver Massey?'

'No.' Maggie wondered how much worse she could feel. 'Your father wouldn't do anything that might reflect badly on you. He was prepared to wait until the statutory two years were up to get his freedom. That was why you knew nothing about it. There was no big scandal, no media circus, as there no doubt would have been if the truth had ever come out.'

'Oh, Mum,' said Lindsey again, and Maggie made a sound of self-derision.

'I know,' she said. 'It wasn't a good time for me. When I first got the letter from your father's solicitors, I went to see him. I begged him to forgive me, but he told me he never wanted to lay eyes on me again.'

Lindsey looked puzzled. 'But you got custody of me.'

'Yes. Ironic, wasn't it?' Maggie gave her a fleeting look. 'By keeping the divorce civil, he couldn't accuse me of adultery. You'll discover courts usually find in favour of the mother.'

'I see.'

'Of course, your father never contested it,' added Maggie, sighing. 'Perhaps he thought I'd learned my lesson; and I had. Whatever, he paid for the house in Prince's Crescent, and made me a generous allowance for you. I have to admit I enjoyed making him pay—for the house.'

'Bitterness?'

'Bitterness,' agreed Maggie. 'And resentment, and humiliation. He was so—so cold, so unforgiving. He wouldn't listen to anything I had to say. If it wasn't for you, I'd never have known what he was doing. He certainly never tried to keep in touch.'

'And now?'

'Well...' Maggie's cheeks were suddenly bright with colour. 'You know why I came to see him. What more is there to say?' She paused. 'I suppose you despise me for not telling you before. I used to tell myself there wasn't much point, but I suppose I was only avoiding the truth.'

'I don't despise you.' Lindsey gave her a reassuring look. 'I'm not saying I don't wish you'd told me before, but I don't honestly see what bearing it has on what's happening today. Except that I think you've both been very silly. It's not something I'd break up my marriage for.' She grimaced. 'That's always supposing I get married. Right now, it's not even on the cards.'

CHAPTER TWELVE

NEIL didn't appear at lunchtime.

When Maggie came downstairs after taking a shower, it was to find only her daughter and Luke Parry in the morning room. They were discussing whether or not it was wise to take the horses out in the snow, and Luke was explaining that although they'd take no harm from being exercised in the yard any prolonged activity would have to wait until the roads were at least partially cleared and there was no danger of them falling and breaking a leg.

'Did you have a good swim?' he enquired as Maggie joined them at the table, and she made an effort to sound enthusiastic.

'It was good,' she said, flashing an anxious glance towards her daughter. 'The water was really warm, and after working out in the gym it helped to ease the aches and pains.'

'You don't have any aches and pains, do you, Mum?' asked Lindsey, proving that their conversation had not caused any lasting damage.

'Just a few,' said Maggie ruefully. 'But nothing I can't handle.'

'I must admit I enjoy swimming,' put in Luke, rubbing his injured knee with an involuntary hand. 'And in the summer Neil slides the windows back and it's almost as good as an outdoor pool.'

'Better,' said Lindsey firmly, giving them both a confident smile. 'After all, you can't use an outdoor pool all winter.' She paused. 'Tomorrow, I'm going to use the sauna as well.'

Maggie tried not to reveal her excitement. After the

morning she had had, it would have been far too easy to
let her relief show. And, although she wasn't looking forward to the prospect, she was going to have to let Neil
know what Lindsey had said. She might be making a moun-
tain out of a molehill, but the girl had said she didn't want
to get married—a complete about-face from her view of
just a few days before. Surely that was to their advantage?
It certainly wouldn't seem to be an advantage to Mike
Reynolds.

'Aren't we waiting for Daddy?' Lindsey exclaimed, as
Mrs Fenwick came bustling into the room, carrying a soup
tureen. The delicious aroma of beef consommé came to
Maggie's nostrils as the woman set the dish on the table,
but it was marred somewhat by Lindsey's troubled expression.

'I expect he's having lunch at Mrs Braithwaite's,' answered the housekeeper comfortably, totally unaware of the
reaction her words evoked. 'There,' she said, taking the lid
off the tureen. 'It's hot and rich and wholesome. Just what
you all need on a day as cold as this.'

Lindsey's lips set in a mutinous line. 'I'm not hungry,'
she muttered, propping her elbows on the table. 'Anyway,
how come she turned up today, when all the roads are supposed to be blocked?' she added, echoing the thought
Maggie had had earlier. 'She doesn't have her own snow-
plough, does she?'

'Bless you, no.' Mrs Fenwick chuckled, not at all put out
by Lindsey's sulky face. And, although Maggie sensed
Luke's sudden stiffening beside her, she went on, without
hesitation, 'As she just lives in the dower house, she doesn't
have far to come.'

'The dower house!' echoed Maggie, losing her appetite
as well, and Luke sighed.

'She had nowhere to live when she came back to
Bellthorpe,' he explained awkwardly. 'Her father didn't
want her at the farm, what—what with—' He cast a hopeful
glance at Mrs Fenwick, but if that lady understood his discomfort she didn't show it, and he was forced to go on.
'What with—Mrs Barlow, and all.' He cleared his throat,
and then continued, with even less conviction, 'The dower

house was empty, and Neil was looking for a tenant. It seemed—the decent thing to do to let Nicola live there.'

'The dower house!' Lindsey repeated her mother's exclamation, and Maggie could tell she was even more shocked than she was. 'But that's *our* house. I'd rather she didn't live on the estate at all. I don't even like her.'

'Lindsey!'

Maggie was unhappily aware that the housekeeper was listening to every word, and Luke, too, was now regarding the girl with some disapproval. 'I don't think it matters whether you like her or not,' he declared, attempting to rescue the situation. He forced a smile. 'Um—thank you, Mrs Fenwick. We'll let you know when we're finished.'

'I'm finished now,' stated Lindsey, giving him her most scornful look. 'And you can tell Daddy when you see him that I didn't come here so he could spend all his time with his girlfriend. If he's bored with us already, then perhaps he shouldn't have invited us.'

'Oh, I don't think—' began Luke in dismay, but Lindsey had beaten Mrs Fenwick out of the door. They heard her footsteps as she crossed the hall, and then silence as she went up the carpeted stairs.

The silence she left behind was even more eloquent. Mrs Fenwick, who had already been on her way, delivered a rueful smile before following Lindsey out of the door, and Maggie twisted her hands together in her lap. Damn Neil, she thought uncharitably; damn him for causing so much trouble. Wasn't it enough that he should humiliate her? Did he have to upset their daughter as well?

Luke sniffed, obviously disturbed by what had happened, and struggled manfully to make amends. 'I thought you knew,' he muttered tersely, though she was sure he hadn't thought that at all. 'For God's sake, Maggie, you knew that they were friends.'

'Friends?'

Maggie gave him an old-fashioned look, and saw the colour enter his pale face. 'Yes, friends,' he averred staunchly. 'And you can't blame him because she turned up uninvited. Equally, he couldn't let her go back on her own.'

'Nicola said he'd phoned her.'

'So?'

'So, according to her, he was desperate to see her.' She lifted her shoulders. 'It doesn't matter to me; I just wish he'd consider Lindsey's feelings, that's all.'

'He does consider Lindsey's feelings,' protested Luke. 'Maggie, he's spent the last three or four days humouring her. If their relationship isn't strong enough to cope with another influence, you have to ask yourself if it's strong enough to survive.'

Maggie looked at him uncertainly. 'Do you think it is?'

'I always did.' Luke's eyes widened with obvious meaning, and she realised it wasn't just Lindsey's relationship with Neil he was talking about. 'He loved you both, Maggie. And, dammit, he trusted you. Why the hell did you let that oaf, Massey, come between you?'

Maggie blinked, startled by the sudden switch from defence to attack. 'I didn't.'

'Didn't you?' Luke considered her for a moment longer, and then seemed to decide he had said enough. Picking up the ladle, he began to serve some of the soup into a bowl. 'Come on,' he said. 'Let's eat. It's delicious. I can vouch for that.'

Maggie wasn't hungry, but she agreed to try some, for Mrs Fenwick's benefit, if nothing else, and she found it was easier to swallow after the first mouthful. She didn't have any of the crusty bread, but the vegetables in the soup were filling, and by the time the housekeeper returned to collect the plates she could honestly say she had enjoyed it.

They had coffee at the table, purposefully avoiding all controversial topics. Afterwards, Maggie excused herself, with the prime objective of going to look for Lindsey. She knew where her daughter's room was now; in fact, she had a fairly good idea of the layout of all the rooms. And she was eager to find her daughter and reassure her of her father's affection.

But, in the event, Lindsey wasn't in her room.

Maggie was instantly concerned. After the way the girl had left the table, it was all too easy to imagine her storm-

ing out into the snow. When she was angry, Lindsey could
be reckless, and she cursed Neil again for being the cause
of her distress.

Realising she couldn't relax until she knew where her
daughter was, Maggie marched along to her own room to
don an extra sweater over her shirt. She didn't stop to
change into warm trousers. Her skirt was long and thick,
and she was wearing thick stockings. She didn't have any
rubber boots, so her leather ones had to suffice. They might
not be waterproof, she reflected ruefully, but they were
more serviceable than her shoes.

When she stepped outside a few minutes later, she realised again how cosseted they were inside the house. Fires,
and central heating, had given her an artificial impression
of the temperature outside, and she was glad she had put
on the extra sweater under her coat.

Someone—Mr Fenwick, she surmised—had cleaned a
path right round the house. Maggie knew, from what
Lindsey had told her, that the stables were situated away
from the house itself, and she had already decided to make
them her first objective.

Around the side of the house, a cobbled yard gave access
to a collection of sheds and outbuildings. The huge garage
block was attached to the house by means of a breezeway,
and Maggie's eyes were drawn to the windows of Luke's
apartment which was situated above. She still hadn't taken
him up on his offer of a guided tour, she remembered. But
since that time when Neil had come to her bedroom she
had avoided any private conversations with Luke, or anyone else.

Right now, all she could think about was Lindsey, and
the worrying possibility of where she might be. Although
she told herself that her daughter was perfectly capable of
looking after herself, this was unfamiliar territory for both
of them.

The route to the stables led past the kitchen garden, and
a row of hothouses, through a copse of ash and alder, and
between a pair of railed paddocks. Snow lay thickly against
the north side of the fences, where the wind had caused
drifting during the night. But the path itself was worn down

into a hard track, which, while being slippery in places, was nevertheless passable.

She could hear voices, and sense the activity at the stables, before she reached the stable yard. When she rounded the corner of the barn, she found two horses stamping around on the forecourt, with a youth of perhaps Lindsey's age attempting to hold onto a lunge rein. She guessed this was the boy Lindsey had spoken of, the one who wanted to train to be a vet. But it was the man bending to examine one of the horse's legs that drew Maggie's eyes. So, she thought, Neil wasn't at the dower house after all.

As if sensing they were no longer alone, he straightened at that moment, and met Maggie's eyes across the horse's back. Then, patting the animal's flank, he turned to the youth and said, 'I don't think there's any swelling there, Tim. But we'll keep an eye on her, anyway.'

The boy nodded, and then, seeing Maggie, he too acknowledged her presence. His smile was friendly, and she could quite see why Lindsey might be taken with him. At a little under six feet, with broad shoulders and dark curly hair, he was one of the most good-looking youths Maggie had ever seen.

'Were you looking for me, Maggie?'

Neil's enquiry was civil enough, but she sensed he wasn't as calm as he appeared. What was the matter? she wondered. Had Nicola been giving him a hard time because of what she and Lindsey had said? Or was he just annoyed because she'd come down here without being asked?

'Actually, I was looking for Lindsey,' she replied, looking at the youth as she spoke. It occurred to her that he might know more than Neil. It depended how long her ex-husband had been here.

'Lindsey?' Neil's dark brows descended. 'Isn't she up at the house?'

'If she were, I wouldn't be looking for her,' retorted Maggie somewhat tersely. And then smiled at the boy to show that she wasn't losing her temper.

Neil frowned. 'Well, she's not been down here, has she, Tim?' His lips tightened. 'By the way, this is Tim Fitzgerald, Harry Fitzgerald's son. He farms—'

'Farther up the valley. I know. Ben Armstrong told me.' Maggie earned herself a scowling look. 'Hello, Tim. Lindsey mentioned you were working here.'

'Hello, Mrs Jordan.' Evidently her daughter hadn't told him that her mother had reverted to her unmarried name. 'Do you think Lindsey's gone out in the snow?'

'I don't know where she's gone,' Maggie declared, biting her lip. 'I suppose I'd better think of where else that could be.'

'Are you saying you have some reason for thinking she's gone out?' demanded Neil. And then, with an impatient look at the youth, he said, 'Come into the office for a moment. Abbott's away, so we won't be disturbed.'

'Oh, I—' Maggie hesitated, cast a look at Tim's discreetly averted head, and then followed her husband into the barn. It wouldn't do to create a scene in front of the boy, she decided, sighing. He might just mention it to Lindsey, and she didn't want that.

The office, which was adjacent to a row of stalls, smelt of leather and grain, and a distinctive scent compounded of disinfectant and horse sweat. Saddles were hung on the walls, and a collection of bits and bridles were strewn on the bench below them. There was a desk, and a worn leather chair, and a pile of horse blankets were stacked near the door.

'Now,' said Neil, without inviting her to sit down, 'd'you want to tell me what's going on?'

Maggie held up her head. 'Don't speak to me like that!' she exclaimed. 'I haven't done anything wrong.'

Neil made an obvious effort to keep his temper. 'Meaning I have?'

'Well, that depends on your point of view, I suppose,' Maggie declared tartly. 'How long has your girlfriend been living at the dower house?'

'Ah.'

Neil's lips twisted, and Maggie wanted to strangle him. 'Yes, "ah",' she said. 'And you couldn't expect Lindsey to be delighted by the news, could you? Not when it used to be *our* home.'

'It was never *our* home,' he replied, after a moment.

'You were never happy there, and it holds no sentimental memories for me.' He paused. 'Are you sure it was Lindsey who was upset that Nicola was living there? How did she find out, anyway? Has Luke been opening his big mouth again?'

'It was Mrs Fenwick, actually,' said Maggie shortly, resenting the fact that he'd immediately put her into the position of having to defend herself. 'When you didn't join us for lunch, Lindsey asked where you were. Your housekeeper assumed that you were having your lunch with your tenant.'

Neil's lips tightened. 'So?'

'So Lindsey left the table without eating her lunch.' Maggie drew a breath. 'Look, can we resume this conversation when we've found her? I'm afraid she might have gone out and got lost in the snow.'

'Unlikely,' said Neil flatly, closing the door and leaning back against it, and Maggie wished she could be as certain as he sounded. 'Where have you looked? The gym? The sauna? The pool area? Luke's apartment? I know she likes to go and sort through all his old 45s.'

Maggie realised she'd looked in none of those places, and as if he knew what she was thinking Neil pulled a mobile phone out of his pocket. Punching in a string of numbers, he put the receiver to his ear, and a second later she heard the distant sound of Luke Parry's voice on the line.

Turning away, so he wouldn't think she was trying to listen in to his conversation, Maggie nevertheless couldn't help hearing what her husband said. 'Luke, we're looking for Lindsey. What? Oh, right, she's with you. That's a relief. I was going to ask you to take a look around the gym.'

Maggie's shoulders sagged. She barely heard how Neil ended the call. The relief she was feeling at knowing Lindsey wasn't out on the moor overwhelmed all else. All the same, she couldn't help feeling annoyed with Luke. He must have guessed she'd go looking for her daughter, but he'd kept Lindsey's whereabouts to himself.

'Don't blame Luke.' Her first awareness that Neil had finished the call was when he spoke. 'I get the impression she isn't too keen on either of us right now. My advice is leave her alone. She'll get over it.'

Maggie was amazed at the strength of the anger that gripped her at that moment. Swinging round, she faced him with none of the apprehension that had troubled her before. 'That's your advice, is it?' she demanded. 'Just leave her alone, and she'll get over it? Of course. That's how you handle all your problems. Leave them to God, and providence, and they might just go away.'

'What brought this on?' Neil eased his shoulders into a more comfortable position against the hard wood. 'I thought you'd be pleased to know she's not in any danger. Or was I the real target all along?'

Maggie controlled her colour with an effort. 'I don't know what you mean.'

'Yes, you do.' Neil wasn't having that. 'You resented the fact that I brought Nicola to the gym. Forget about the dower house. You were already disgruntled over her arrival. Don't bother to deny it. It was obvious.'

Maggie straightened her spine. 'If my reaction didn't meet with your approval I'm sorry. But you're wrong if you think Lindsey can't see for herself what's going on. Perhaps you should ask yourself why she's sought sanctuary with Luke. Hadn't you warned her there was another woman in your life?'

Neil scowled. 'What have you been telling her?'

Maggie didn't want to get into that, and she was sure she must look as guilty as sin. 'Nothing about you,' she muttered stiffly, but without much conviction. 'Now, will you get away from the door? I want to go back to the house.'

Neil didn't move, and his lean features assumed a suspicious expression. 'I don't believe you,' he said. 'You always were a poor liar, Maggie.' His lips twisted. 'Which, I suppose, is why you didn't try to lie to me about your sad affair.'

'What sad affair?'

Neil was mocking. 'You mean there's been more than one?'

Maggie clenched her fists. 'I've never had an affair—

with anyone,' she retorted coldly. 'Now, if you've finished making fun of me, I'd like to leave.'

'I bet you would.' But Neil made no attempt to let her. 'Come on; what have you been telling Lindsey? I mean to find out.'

'Or you'll what?' Maggie demanded, with more vehemence than she'd thought she was capable of showing. 'You can't do much to me with Tim just outside the door.'

'Tim's not there,' he answered laconically, and in the moment it took for her to check his statement and discover he was lying he took hold of her wrist. 'Go on, scream,' he dared her, drawing her towards him. 'See if Tim comes to your rescue.' His brows arched. 'Or just decides it's more than his job's worth.'

Maggie made a sound of frustration. 'Why are you doing this?' she exclaimed, when his free hand slid into her hair. She felt the silky strands spilling around his fingers. 'After what happened in my bedroom, I'd have thought you'd have avoided me like the plague.'

'Would you?' His hand tightened suddenly, his fingertips digging almost painfully into her head. 'Well, I've been wanting to talk to you about that. But I got the impression you were avoiding me.'

Maggie stared at him with all the resentment she could muster. 'Do you blame me?' she countered coldly. 'I'm not a toy you can pick up at will, Neil. I don't understand what you're trying to prove.'

'That you're still crazy about me, I suppose,' he remarked, his hand sliding infuriatingly down to her neck. And as his words caused an instinctive stiffening he added, 'Don't try to deny it. You didn't exactly fight me off the other day.'

Maggie gasped. 'How dare you? I was trying to get away from you when I fell.'

'Ah, but then you became as sexy as a pussy-cat. It would have taken a better man than me to turn you down.'

'You liar!' Maggie was incensed. 'You can't pretend you were indifferent to—to our making love.'

'But we weren't making love, were we?' Neil taunted her, restraining her efforts to get away from him with his free hand. 'It was sex, pure and simple, Mags, and you know it. Or not so pure, as it happened. Did Massey teach you all those dirty things you said?'

'You bastard!'

Maggie felt the tears spring to her eyes at his cruel disparagement of something she had secretly cherished. Despite everything that had happened, she had foolishly believed that Neil couldn't have made love to her as he had without feeling something for her too. What they had shared had been so beautiful, in spite of all the torment that had gone before. She realised she had avoided mentioning it until now because she hadn't wanted to shatter her stupid dreams.

But Neil's words destroyed any hopes she might have been nurturing, and all she could think of was getting away before he said anything else. Instinct took over, and with an impulse born of panic she brought her knee up between his legs. She didn't care just then if she hurt him; her whole focus was on herself. If she'd stopped to think, she wouldn't have done it, but her emotions were rioting out of control.

Her knee barely skimmed its target. As luck would have it, Neil was straightening away from the door as she struck, and a hasty twist of his body blocked her worst assault. Instead, he muttered a savage oath and, swinging her about, thrust her shoulders back against the door. 'You crazy idiot! You could have gelded me,' he muttered, imprisoning her there with the weight of his body. 'My God, is this what we've come to? A nasty little scuffle in the barn!'

Maggie was trembling now. The realisation of what she had tried to do made her feel weak with loathing, not for him but for herself, and the pitiful creature she had become. What had she hoped to achieve by attacking him? Had she forgotten it was supposed to be for Lindsey that she was here?

'I'm sorry,' she said unsteadily, the prolonged pressure of his heavy frame against her reducing her breathing to a shallow gulp for air. 'You—it was what you said, the things you accused me of; I know you don't believe me, but I never had a relationship with Oliver Massey. I admitted that—that once I—I went to bed with him. But it wasn't what I wanted, whatever you choose to think.'

She doubted he was listening to her. As she spoke, as she struggled desperately to justify something that he hadn't wanted to hear about more than five years ago, and certainly wouldn't want to hear about now, Neil's anger was dissipating. His mouth, which only moments before had been tight and thin-lipped with fury, was softening, gentling, taking on a distinctly sensual curve, and she knew, without being told, what he was thinking. He wasn't thinking about Oliver Massey, or, if he was, he was prepared to put it aside for the present. He was remembering a different scene, and the blood rushed hotly to her face.

'No, Neil.'

'No?' He said the word, but it didn't mean anything. Like her, he was increasingly aware of the undoubted intimacy of their situation, and although he lifted his hands to brace them against the door at either side of her head he didn't attempt to lift his weight from her. On the contrary, he began to move against her, rotating his hips deliberately against her lower body, making her over- whelmingly aware of what he was doing to her, and the sudden ache that flowered between her legs.

'No,' she said again, realising that allowing this to go on was not going to win her any favours. At the end of the day, he would only despise her even more than he did already, and although she might console herself with the fact that he still wanted her it was a sexual need at best. 'Neil, you can't!'

'Oh, I think I must,' he answered thickly, this time hearing the entreating note in her tone. 'God, Maggie, d'you know what you do to me? Have you any idea how crazy you make me feel?'

Maggie thought she might, but when she tried to answer him Neil covered her mouth with his. His tongue plunged between her teeth, and she was imprisoned in a world of pure sensation where the only thing that mattered was that its hot, wet possession of her mouth should go on and on.

Her senses swam as he bit her lips, and sucked her tongue, and drove her almost wild with the kisses he rained

all over her face. Her nose, her cheeks, her temple—all
tingled with the urgent pressure of his lips. Her eyelids felt
heavy, and she had to fight to keep her languid eyes open.
It would be so easy to succumb to her sensual needs.

And while he scattered her senses with his mouth his
hands tore open the buttons on her coat, and, pushing it off
her shoulders, deposited it, like so much excess baggage,
at her feet. She wanted to protest, to say it was the only
cashmere coat she had, and it wouldn't take kindly to the
straw and grain that had been trodden into the office floor
by unwary feet, but she couldn't voice the words. Besides,
for all her silent protests, her resistance was becoming
weaker. Neil had always had this effect on her, and it was
no defence to know that she affected him too.

His jacket was parted, and now that her coat was off she
could feel the accelerated beat of his heart against her chest.
She believed him when he said she made him crazy. It was
the only reason she could think of for his uncharacteristic
loss of control.

She brought up her hands almost tentatively. When he'd
made love to her in her bedroom, she had tried not to touch
him, but now the need to feel his skin beneath her hands
overcame everything else. With a strength she hadn't
known she possessed, she pulled the sides of his shirt apart,
spreading her palms against his heat and revelling in the
fine dark hair that sprang beneath her fingertips.

'God, Maggie!'

She had no doubt that what she was doing disturbed Neil
as much as herself. When she ran her caressing hands
across his chest, he shuddered uncontrollably, and against
her stomach she felt the throbbing hardness that disclosed
his need. She couldn't prevent the urge to touch that raw
exposure, and her fingers closed around him though the
cloth of his trousers.

It wasn't until later that she realised how reckless they
had been. Right then, the fact that opposite the door there
was a long low window didn't worry her, nor the fact that
someone—Tim, for instance—might look through it and
see what was going on. Granted, the window was grimy.
The amount of dust that was scattered both inside and out-

side the building made that almost a given. But nevertheless it was accessible, if anyone was curious enough to look.

But at that moment Maggie wasn't thinking of anything but her own needs, her own senses. When Neil pushed her sweater up to her shoulders, and bent his head to suckle at her breasts, she didn't stop him. Even when he got impatient because her bra wasn't front-fastening this time, and tore the flimsy elastic with his hand, she didn't object. Her whole body was arching towards its own fulfilment, and Neil was not immune to her response.

She had a momentary bite of self-consciousness, when he grasped her skirt and pushed it up to her waist. God, she thought, he couldn't intend to take her here, against the door, could he? But it seemed he could, as his fingers fumbled impatiently for his zip. A moment later, the heat and strength of his erection pressed against the bared swell of her stomach. She glanced down—she couldn't help herself—and saw the bead of moisture on its tip. Almost involuntarily, it seemed, she allowed her finger to rescue that drop of moisture, but when she raised her finger to her lips Neil went totally wild.

'God, Maggie,' he groaned, cupping his hands beneath her bottom and lifting her weight, so that she was sandwiched between him and the door. Then, with shaking hands, he lowered her onto him, filling her with such exquisite completeness that she couldn't deny the moan that escaped her throat.

It wasn't like before. Neil was hungry for her, and his thrusts were slick and powerful, and fiercely intent. With half-closed eyes, and sweat beading on his forehead, he swiftly brought them both to an incredible summit of pleasure and then drove them over the brink with a final, soul-wrenching force.

When he lowered her to the floor, Maggie wasn't sure that her legs would support her. Although she had had them curled about Neil's waist as he drove into her, now they were weak and shaking with the feelings that had gripped her. What she would have really liked to do was lie down, and the horse blankets stacked beside the door were unreasonably appealing. She was exhausted; she just wanted to curl up and go to sleep.

But it was the sight of the horse blankets that brought her to her senses, and to the awareness of how recklessly she had behaved. Not only that, she was ashamed to be standing there, with her breasts exposed and her skirt pushed up around her waist. For all Neil's jeans were around his ankles, he didn't look half so abandoned, she thought.

And, while she thrust down her sweater, feeling the torn edges of her bra prick her skin, and bent to pull up her panties, all he had to do was haul up his jeans and fasten his zip. While she struggled to restore her skirt to order, he simply lounged in front of her, fastening the buttons on his shirt, his eyes totally unreadable in his lean, sensual face.

Her coat took rather more trouble. As she'd suspected, it had collected a covering of dust and straw. Looking at it, anyone would have thought they had used it as a blanket, she thought painfully. Perhaps if they had she wouldn't be feeling so abused now.

'Can I go?' she asked at last, after brushing the worst of the damage from her coat, and Neil seemed to recover his earlier mood.

'Why not?' he asked. 'I don't suppose this is a good time for us to continue our conversation.' He viewed her tightly drawn features. 'D'you want an apology?'

'From you?'

Maggie's voice broke. She could hear it, and as if aware of her splintering control Neil heaved a sigh. 'Look, Mags,' he said. 'Whether you believe me or not, this wasn't meant to happen. But—' he raked agitated fingers through his thick dark hair '—you get me so mad sometimes, I guess I just lost my head.'

'It doesn't matter.'

'It does matter.'

His hand came to rest at the back of his neck, and she wished her eyes weren't immediately drawn to his sensuous mouth. There was something almost carnal about the way he chewed on his lower lip, and she couldn't forget the way it had made her feel.

'I've got to go,' she said, almost panicking in her need to get away from him. 'I just hope Tim didn't get curious, and come to see where we were. I can just imagine what he'd have thought if he'd looked through that window. I suggest you get some curtains if you plan on doing this with Nicola.'

Neil's eyes darkened. 'You have to strike out, don't you, Maggie? It's not enough that I've told you you drive me crazy. You still have to make stupid remarks like that to turn the screw.'

'I don't screw people,' retorted Maggie, leaving him to work out her meaning, and, wrenching open the door, she strode out with as much dignity as she could find.

CHAPTER THIRTEEN

MAGGIE stiffened.

Someone was playing the piano in the drawing room. She could hear it clearly as she came down the stairs, and although it was a much more melodious rendition she recognised it as one of Neil's own compositions, which he had originally written for the guitar.

She remembered the title, too. Neil had chosen it to celebrate the fact that she was going to have a child. 'Long Night's Loving', she mouthed silently. God, how young they had been in those days. She had no doubt that Neil was playing it for her. But why tonight? Why now?

Unless...

She moistened her dry lips. Unless he was speculating about what had happened. Could he conceivably be hoping she was pregnant again? She shook her head. She didn't believe it. Neil wasn't that fanciful. Besides, if he had another child, it wouldn't be with her.

All the same, she came down the final few stairs with rather more haste than discretion, and crossed the hall to the drawing-room door on hurried feet. But when she appeared in the open doorway her feelings took a sudden tumble. It wasn't Neil sitting at the piano. It was Luke.

'Oh!'

The exclamation couldn't be silenced, and although she doubted he could have heard her Luke looked up. 'Hey, Maggie,' he said. 'You look nice.'

Maggie forced her pulse to steady. 'Thanks,' she said, trying not to look as disappointed as she felt. It was crazy after the way he'd treated her, but she couldn't deny that she'd dressed with Neil in mind. The particular green of her long-skirted dress had been one of his favourites, and the V-neckline and long, tight sleeves gave it an almost medieval appearance.

Luke got up from the piano. 'Can I get you a drink?' he asked, crossing to the table where the tray of drinks was situated. 'As we're the first, we might as well take advantage of the fact.'

Maggie ventured into the room. 'Um—white wine would be nice,' she agreed, positioning herself near the fire. 'And thanks for talking to Lindsey this afternoon. She told me you'd—well, put her mind at rest.'

Luke handed her a glass of wine. 'I only told her the truth,' he protested honestly. 'She seemed to think her father was on the point of marrying Nicola Braithwaite. I simply explained that it wasn't so.'

Maggie took a tentative sip of her wine. 'It's not?' she queried, trying to sound only mildly interested, and Luke swallowed a mouthful of his Scotch before shaking his head.

'They're good friends,' he said firmly. 'They've known one another for years. Well, you know that, Maggie. And Neil's in no hurry to—to—'

'Make another mistake?' suggested Maggie drily, but Luke only gave her a reproving glance.

'Was it a mistake?' he asked. 'I always thought you and Neil were ideally suited. If it hadn't been for—well, for what happened, it would never have got as far as a divorce.'

Maggie was tempted to continue the discussion. It was interesting hearing someone else's viewpoint, even if Luke was as biased in Neil's favour as Jackie was in hers. At least he didn't seem to hold a grudge towards her, whereas Jackie put Neil down every chance she got.

But it didn't seem right to discuss Neil in his own house, and there was always the possibility that he could walk into the room at any moment. Besides, she still wasn't precisely sure what Neil wanted of her. It would be so easy to fool herself into thinking he was prepared to give her a second chance.

Lindsey breezed into the room a few moments later, making Maggie glad she hadn't succumbed to the urge to be indiscreet. She was far too grateful for the tenuous relationship she had formed with her daughter, and she wanted nothing to jeopardise it.

Lindsey, too, had taken trouble with her appearance. For once, she was wearing a dress, an ankle-length pinafore that Maggie had brought her from the shop. It was black—Lindsey's choice, not hers—but she was wearing a white ribbed sweater underneath. Even her shoes were the squat-heeled platforms Maggie had bought for her at Christmas, instead of the clunky boots she invariably wore.

'Cool,' said Luke, using Lindsey's own expression, and she gave him a mocking grin.

'I can wear skirts if I have to,' she announced, going across to the drinks tray. 'Can I have a glass of wine too?'

'I don't see why not.'

Luke poured, and Maggie felt a little of the tension she had been feeling disperse. It was going to be all right, she told herself. Despite the weather, coming up here had been for the best.

'Daddy's invited Tim to join us for supper,' Lindsey added, sipping her wine as she came to join her mother on the sofa. She gave Maggie a defensive look and hunched her shoulders. 'It wasn't my idea,' she protested. 'Daddy seems to think I enjoy his company.'

'And don't you?' asked Maggie, mentally revising the reasons why her daughter had chosen to put on a dress. She wondered what Neil had said to Lindsey. Whatever it was, they were apparently speaking again.

'He's all right.' Lindsey answered her question offhandedly. 'He's a bit immature, but so long as Mike's in London...'

Her voice trailed away, but Maggie got the feeling she wasn't missing Mike Reynolds as much as perhaps she thought she should. In any event, she was not averse to enjoying another male's company, which reminded Maggie that she had still not told Neil what Lindsey had said in the gym.

Not that she had had much opportunity, she admitted half-irritably, aware that she had not conducted herself with any merit that afternoon. What was it about Neil that drove her to behave with such abandon? Particularly after his callous disregard of her feelings.

No matter what Luke said, she was not convinced that Neil's relationship with Nicola Braithwaite was as casual as he seemed to think. Apart from anything else, she knew Nicola of old, and she couldn't believe that she just wanted a friend.

Neil himself joined them a few minutes later. Although he wasn't wearing an evening suit, the black jacket and trousers were more formal than usual, and for once he was wearing a tie. The fact that the tie was pulled away from his collar, and the top button of his shirt was unfastened, rather ruined the image, yet somehow he managed to look even more disturbing than ever.

'You'll be pleased to hear that they expect to have the main road completely cleared by morning,' he said as Luke went to pour him a drink. 'It was on the local news at six o'clock.'

Lindsey got to her feet. 'Does that mean we'll be leaving?' she asked, and Maggie couldn't decide whether the girl was pleased or not.

'It means that they expect to have the main road cleared by morning,' repeated her father drily. 'You're welcome to stay as long as your mother permits.'

Lindsey frowned, and glanced round at Maggie. 'Oh, then I suppose we will be going home. I'm surprised Aunt Jackie hasn't been on the phone before now. She always seems to run into some problem if Mum isn't around.'

'Jackie doesn't have this phone number,' remarked Neil, with a slight smile, and Maggie realised that was true. Although she had rung her sister when it had become obvious that the snow was going to be a problem, she had had to leave a message on her answering machine, and it was only now that she understood why her sister hadn't replied.

'Hey, great!' said Lindsey, grinning, clearly pleased that this was the case. But then she frowned. 'I suppose that means Mike doesn't have this number either. He won't be able to get in touch with me when he gets back.'

Neil was saved from having to answer this by the sound

of the doorbell. Guessing it must be Tim Fitzgerald, Lindsey accompanied her father into the hall. Which gave Maggie a breathing space to reassess the situation, and to try and come to terms with what she was going to do.

So far this evening, Neil hadn't even spoken to her, but she'd been intensely aware of his presence ever since he'd walked into the room. However much she might despise the fact, where he was concerned she seemed to have no defences. She didn't know what his intentions were, unless this was his way of taking his revenge.

The sound of voices in the hall forced her to school her features into a polite mask, but the sight of Nicola Braithwaite, preceding her daughter into the room, caused her to catch her breath. It appeared that Neil had invited another guest, to even the numbers, but Maggie wished fervently now that she had had some excuse to avoid coming down for supper.

The fact that Tim Fitzgerald followed Lindsey into the room was little compensation. Apparently, he and Nicola had met on the doorstep, and at least his presence diverted Lindsey's attention from her father. For her part, Maggie wondered if Neil expected her to partner Luke. Whatever, he had successfully succeeded in destroying the evening, so far as she was concerned.

Unable to sit still while Nicola behaved as if she was already the mistress of the house, Maggie left the sofa and walked across to the piano. Seating herself on the stool, she pretended to have some interest in the sheet music set upon the stand, lingering over the tune Luke had been playing, even though it seemed sentimental in retrospect. It was impossible to go back, she thought wistfully. She was only building up more heartbreak for herself by even imagining she could. What she'd done, she'd done, and there was no making any better of it. Neil might find her sexually attractive, but he was just using her to assuage a purely physical need.

She was aware of someone coming to join her, and, expecting it to be Luke, she glanced up with a rueful smile. 'This song must be nearly twenty years old—' she'd begun before she realised it wasn't Luke who was now edging onto the stool beside her, but her ex-husband.

'Well, eighteen years old,' he amended drily. 'We're not quite as old as that.' His thigh had trapped her skirt, successfully keeping her there beside him. 'I like your dress. I've always liked you in green.'

Maggie kept her gaze on the music. 'What a pity I'd forgotten,' she remarked tersely, and she heard him give a lazy laugh. 'Aren't you afraid you'll be accused of neglecting your lady friend? You should have told her of your preference. I'm sure she'd have been more than happy to wear anything you asked.'

Neil was unperturbed. 'I said I liked *you* in green,' he remarked, his gaze barely flicking over Nicola's black-clad figure as she stood listening, with evident impatience, to whatever it was Luke was telling her. Clearly, she considered Neil should be entertaining her, whatever he thought. 'Of course, it's more fun taking your clothes off,' he added huskily. 'Have you forgiven me for what happened this afternoon?'

Maggie swallowed a sip of her wine, holding the glass with both hands so that the tremor in her fingers wouldn't show. 'I don't think you want my forgiveness,' she said, when she felt capable of answering him. 'I think what you really want to do is remind me of it. To embarrass me here—now—in front of your friends.'

Neil's mouth compressed. 'D'you really think I'd do a thing like that?'

Maggie risked a fleeting glance at his face. 'Wouldn't you?'

His eyes darkened. 'If I wanted to embarrass you, I'd do a much better job of it,' he assured her harshly. 'What is it with you, Maggie? Can't you accept the fact that you still want me?'

'I don't still want you,' she contradicted him swiftly, but it was just an automatic response to his arrogance. Despite everything that had happened, she couldn't remember a time when she hadn't wanted him. Even when she'd thought she hated him, she'd still been unable to get the thought of him out of her head.

Neil shrugged. 'Have it your own way,' he said flatly, but she thought she glimpsed a certain tightening about his mouth. Not that she imagined he was hurt by her remark, only irritated. He wanted to believe he could still pull her strings.

'Anyway,' she said, after a moment, realising this might be the only opportunity she'd have of talking to him this evening, 'I—I forgot to tell you something Lindsey said to me this morning.' She paused, wishing she weren't so aware of him beside her. 'Um—she said that so far as she's concerned marriage isn't an option.'

Neil seemed to take a moment to absorb what she had said, and then remarked, somewhat curtly, 'To Reynolds, you mean?'

'To anyone,' said Maggie, aware that she had expected a more positive reaction. 'She told me that at present it's not even on the cards.'

'I see.' Neil was silent for a moment. 'And she just told you this, out of the blue?'

'Well, no.' That was harder. 'We—er—we were talking about marriage—about getting married.' She stopped trying to justify herself, and added, 'I thought you'd be as relieved as I am at the news.'

'Oh, I am.' But Neil didn't look relieved. 'But when you say you were talking about marriage, is that marriage in general, or our marriage in particular?'

Maggie felt the heat invade her neck. 'Does it matter?'

'I think so.' Neil sucked in a breath. 'How much have you told her about us?'

Maggie buried her nose in her wineglass, but Neil wasn't about to let her off the hook. Even though he must have been aware that Nicola was scowling at him from across the room, he made no attempt to get up from his seat.

'Everything,' she mumbled at last, realising he could hardly attack her in front of his guests. 'I decided she was old enough to hear the truth.'

Neil's stare had an almost tangible force. '*You* decided?' he echoed harshly. 'Don't you think you should have discussed it with me first?'

'Perhaps.' Maggie conceded the point. 'But she was

starting to ask questions. Would you rather I'd let her think
that you were to blame?'

Neil's hot breath fanned her cheek. 'Perhaps I was,' he
said, and Maggie's breathing was suddenly suspended. 'If
I hadn't insisted on moving up here, Massey would never
have stood a chance of getting near you.'

Maggie struggled for words. 'I've told you—'

'I know.' Neil was bitter. 'He never meant anything to
you.'

'He didn't.'

'Then why the hell did you stay with him after I found
out?'

Maggie gasped. 'I didn't!'

She was almost speechless with disbelief that he should
even think such a thing of her, but as she turned her horrified eyes in Neil's direction the doorbell echoed again
from the hall.

'We're popular tonight,' remarked Luke as Neil was
forced to go and see who it was, and Maggie remained at
the piano, feeling as if she had suddenly gone numb.

'Are you all right, Mum?' Neil's departure, however reluctant, had opened the way for Lindsey to come and join
her. Slipping onto the stool beside her, the girl regarded
her with anxious eyes. 'You look awful,' she added can-
didly. 'What did Daddy say?'

Maggie gazed at her blankly. 'I—I don't know,' she
replied at last, realising she didn't know exactly what Neil
had said. It was all so confusing; the thing he'd accused
her of didn't make sense. She had never stayed with Oliver
Massey, neither before she'd confessed the truth to Neil nor
after.

'Well, whatever it was, you've certainly upset someone,'
declared Lindsey smugly. 'Mrs Braithwaite has been practically spitting blood. I think she suspects you're trying to
get Daddy back, and Luke's been boring her silly with his
plans for the stables.'

Maggie managed a faint smile. 'Good old Luke.'

'Yes, good old Luke,' seconded Lindsey, and then, to
Maggie's dismay, she beckoned Tim over. 'You haven't
met my mother, have you?' she said, as the young man

came to join them, and Maggie wondered if he had any idea how embarrassed she was.

Evidently not. 'We have met actually,' he replied, his grey eyes friendly and filled with nothing but warmth. 'It was just this afternoon, wasn't it, Mrs Jordan?' He looked at Lindsey. 'Your mother came down to the stables looking for you.'

'Of course.' Lindsey saw nothing amiss, and Maggie was sure she was the only one who sensed any restraint in the atmosphere. 'Daddy said he'd phoned from there.' She grinned at her mother. 'Was he showing you the old photographs in the office?'

'I—no.' Maggie didn't know how she controlled her colour. 'We—we were just talking, that's all.' She licked her lips. 'What photographs?' she asked, as if she wanted to know.

'Oh, they're just old lithographs of the racehorses old Miss Cavendish used to own,' Tim was starting to explain, when Lindsey gave a sudden start.

'Mike!' she exclaimed, exchanging a helpless look with her mother, before going to greet the man who had accompanied her father into the drawing room. 'Mike,' she added, not without some hesitation, 'how did you know we were here?'

CHAPTER FOURTEEN

'AND then what happened?'

Jackie's eyes were alight with malicious amusement, and Maggie wished her sister didn't enjoy other people's troubles so openly. It was obvious she was hoping that the story didn't have a happy ending. Hearing that Mike Reynolds had gatecrashed Neil's party could only have one conclusion so far as she was concerned.

'Well, then we had supper,' said Maggie now, getting up from the kitchen table to pour herself another cup of coffee. 'There wasn't much else we could do, short of throwing him out. And with Nicola and Tim as witnesses Neil decided to bite the bullet.'

'I bet he hated having to do that.'

Jackie was positively lapping this up, and Maggie wished she could have avoided the discussion. But, although she'd managed to keep out of her way for the past twenty-four hours, she'd known that sooner or later Jackie was bound to seek her out.

'He didn't stay at the house, did he?' Jackie pressed on, clearly waiting for some sensational revelations. 'I mean, after the way that man's behaved in the past, I imagine you were worried that they might share a bed.'

Maggie shrugged. 'I expect so.'

But although she conceded the point in actuality she had had other, more disturbing things on her mind. Not least what Neil had meant by implying she'd been living with Oliver Massey. Was that what Lindsey had told him? Or someone else?

'Well, go on,' Jackie prompted, growing impatient with

her sister's pensive expression. 'What happened after supper? Was there a row?'

Maggie blew out a breath. 'Not exactly.'

'Maggie!'

'Well, there wasn't.' Maggie regarded the other woman half-defensively. 'Neil's far too subtle for that.'

'So what did he say?'

'Not a lot, to begin with. I think Mike thought that because Neil hadn't immediately turned him out I'd been lying. He certainly behaved as if he had a right to be there.'

Jackie pulled a face. Maggie could tell this wasn't what she had left her flat before eight o'clock in the morning to hear. Particularly when the weather was so unpleasant, and her bed had been so inviting.

'But what about Lindsey?' she exclaimed. 'Didn't he say anything about Lindsey? I can't believe Neil is prepared to let her marry the man.'

'Lindsey doesn't want to marry anyone,' said Maggie with conviction. 'She told me that while we were working out in the gym.'

Jackie gasped. '*You* were working out?' she exclaimed. 'I don't believe it. Since when have you enjoyed getting all hot and sweaty just for fun?'

'I used to,' said Maggie swiftly. 'Before I gave up modelling to have Lindsey. And I like the idea of getting fit again. It's ages since I've done any actual physical exercise at all.'

A thought occurred to her, and she hurriedly lifted her coffee cup to her lips. But the colour that tinted her cheeks was not caused by the heat of the aromatic liquid. It was the memory of that energetic interlude in the stables that had brought the blood rushing to her face.

'And Lindsey told you she didn't want to marry Mike Reynolds?'

Jackie sounded disbelieving, and Maggie couldn't altogether blame her. 'She said she's not thinking of marriage—with anyone,' she amended firmly. 'We had a long talk about—about lots of things, and it came out.'

Jackie's eyes narrowed. 'You and Lindsey had a long talk?' she echoed. 'That must have been a first.'

'Perhaps.' Maggie tried not to resent the implication. 'Anyway, that's what she said and I believe her.'

'And did she tell Mike Reynolds that, too?'

'Well, no.'

'I thought not.'

Jackie was triumphant, and Maggie wondered why she was bothering to explain. Jackie had her own opinion, and she doubted anything she said would change it. She just hoped that Jackie's scepticism didn't influence her daughter. She was far too willing to make her feelings known.

'Anyway,' Maggie said, 'it was Nicola who inadvertently brought things to a head. During supper, she'd been asking Mike about his work—who he represented, that sort of thing.' Maggie grimaced. 'I think she thought Neil would be pleased because she was showing so much interest in the music business, and she obviously assumed that Mike was a friend. He'd called the house, you see, and Mrs Lewis had told him we were in Northumberland. It must have convinced Nicola Mike was a welcome guest.'

'Why not?' Jackie pulled a face. 'The way Lindsey goes on about him, I'd have thought the same.'

Maggie let that go. 'After supper, we had coffee in the drawing room, as usual. Tim was still there, of course, which meant Lindsey didn't spend all her time with Mike. Besides, I really think she likes Tim. I think she was quite embarrassed when Mike came on too strong.'

Jackie arched a speculative brow. 'Really?'

'Yes, really.' Maggie's nostrils flared. 'As I say, she likes Tim. They have a lot in common.'

'What?'

'Their love of horses, for one thing.' Maggie was beginning to get annoyed. 'Why are you being so negative? I'd have thought you'd be glad she'd got a friend of her own age.'

Jackie shrugged, making no comment, and in spite of her resentment Maggie forced herself to continue. 'Nicola had got around to asking about Mike's association with Neil.' She shook her head. 'I suppose that's why he'd come to Haversham, but I don't think he liked her asking awkward questions. Particularly when she involved Neil in the discussion. I think he'd planned to speak to him privately.'

'I'll bet.' Jackie was sardonic. 'Neil wouldn't like that.'

'Well, as a matter of fact, Neil tried to put her off,' declared Maggie crisply. 'He said he'd decided to retire from the record business, and they'd split up. But then Lindsey joined in and said that her father owed Mike a lot, and that's when everything blew up.'

Jackie's interest rekindled. 'How?'

Maggie bit her lip. 'Luke exploded.'

'Luke!'

Jackie was clearly disappointed with this development, but Maggie wasn't interested in her sister's reaction now. 'Yes, Luke,' she said firmly. 'He must have been seething over the fact that Mike had dared to come to Neil's home in the first place. When Lindsey said what she did, he turned on her like a wounded bull.'

Jackie drew back. 'Poor Lindsey,' she observed, but she didn't sound particularly sympathetic.

'Yes, poor Lindsey.' Maggie gave a reminiscent sigh. 'I don't think she thought he had it in him, and it must have given her quite a shock. He was so angry. I think he could have strangled both of them with his bare hands.'

'How dramatic!'

Maggie ignored her sarcasm. 'Yes, it was, actually. Of course, Mike tried to shut him up.' She grimaced. 'So did Neil, as a matter of fact, but Luke was determined to have his say.'

'Are you saying he told her about the money Mike stole from Neil?' Jackie frowned. 'And she believed him?'

'Not at first,' said Maggie honestly, remembering Lindsey's stunned reaction with acute distress. 'After all, Mike was doing his best to refute the accusation, and she was torn between believing him and calling Luke a liar, or vice versa.'

'But dear old Luke won out.' Jackie's lips twisted. 'How sweet.'

'It wasn't like that,' said Maggie wearily. 'You don't understand. Lindsey's always had a special sort of relationship with Luke. For heaven's sake, he was the one who taught her to ride. It hit her hard when he told her what a bastard Mike had been. Until then, I'd been the only one to say a word against him.'

Jackie lifted a shoulder. 'So why hadn't Luke spoken out before this? Had Neil primed him to choose his moment?'

'No.' Maggie was defensive again. 'None of us knew Mike was going to turn up as he did. And until Lindsey made her pitch Luke had no idea what she was thinking.'

Jackie sniffed. 'Well, it all sounds rather dodgy to me. Mike turns up, Luke blows his top, and Lindsey suddenly sees the error of her ways. Honestly, Maggie, you have to admit it does sound very convenient.' She grimaced. 'And they all lived happily ever after! Pardon me while I throw up!'

Maggie held up her head. 'I didn't say they all lived happily ever after,' she defended herself. As far as she was concerned, the ending had been far from ideal. 'Mike left, OK, after Lindsey said she needed some time to think things over, but then she went upstairs to her room, and she's refused to speak to any of us since.'

'And that's a minus?' Jackie was disparaging. 'Maggie, you're only feeling guilty because you've had to come back to town on your own. Well, look at it positively; let her father deal with the situation for once. He's got away without any responsibility for more than five years!'

'That was my choice, not his,' pointed out Maggie quickly. 'You don't imagine Neil wanted to let Lindsey stay with me, do you? Not after finding out about what he assumed to be my ongoing affair.'

Jackie stiffened. 'What has he been saying now?'

'Oh—' Maggie shook her head '—just that he thought Oliver Massey and I were living together, before and after he found out that I'd slept with him. Or, if not actually living together, that I was spending nights at Oliver's apartment. He must have tried to get in touch with me one night when I was staying with you in town. Susan—you remember Susan McNally, Lindsey's nanny?—she must have said something, and he got the wrong impression.'

'As ever,' said Jackie dismissively, pushing her coffee-cup aside. 'It's more likely that Susan told him the truth, but he chose to put his own interpretation on your not being there. You know what he was like, Maggie; he wouldn't listen to a word you said. I hope you're not going to rehash all that misery, just because Neil Jordan chooses to load you with guilt.'

'N-o-o.'

But she was.

Maggie finished her coffee, and got up to wash the dirty cup at the sink. It enabled her to avoid her sister's critical gaze, but she could feel Jackie's eyes boring into her back.

'So...' Jackie seemed to decide it would be wiser not to pursue that particular old chestnut at this moment. 'You said you flew back.' She paused. 'How did you get to the airport?'

'Luke drove me,' replied Maggie, mentally squaring her shoulders. 'As soon as the roads were clear, I made arrangements to catch the evening flight.'

'You came home last night.'

'You know I did.'

'Mmm.' Jackie was thoughtful. 'And you didn't speak to Lindsey before you left?'

'Not about what happened, no.' Maggie braced herself against the drainer. 'I did try to speak to her yesterday, but, as I say, she stayed in her room all day. And when I asked her if she wanted to come home she said she'd rather stay with Neil.'

'But what about school?' exclaimed Jackie impatiently. 'I thought you were concerned about her education.'

'I am.' Maggie glanced pointedly at her watch. 'Heavens, is that the time? Goodness knows what's been happening at the office while I've been away.'

'I'm not entirely useless,' said Jackie shortly, getting up from the table. 'As a matter of fact, the sales figures for December were quite good, and that third shop we've talked about might not be such a distant dream.'

'Oh.' The prospect of taking on the responsibility for a third retail outlet filled Maggie with an uneasy kind of dismay. 'I don't know if we're ready for that, Jackie. Two shops seem more than enough for me.'

Jackie's lips tightened. 'That's not what you said when

we started. And you know very well that the more shops
we have, the more profitable they become.'

Maybe, thought Maggie wearily, but this wasn't the time
to talk about it. She had far too many other things on her
mind. Besides, she no longer had the enthusiasm she had
once had. These past few days with Neil had reminded her
of all she had lost.

'I have to go,' she said, hoping her sister would take the
hint and do the same.

Jackie managed their main shop here in town, and was
overall manager of both shops, even though the one in
Bournemouth seldom required her intervention. She had
never been keen on working in the office, which restricted
her workload considerably. Maggie usually did all the pa-
perwork with the help of her assistant, Lucy Wells.

'When is Lindsey coming back, then?' Jackie asked now,
sliding her arms into the sleeves of her sheepskin coat, and
Maggie sighed.

'I'm not sure,' she said. And she wasn't. 'But I think, in
the circumstances, she deserves a break.'

'Don't we all?' remarked her sister sardonically, evidently waiting for Maggie to put on her coat. 'Come on,
Maggie, Mrs Lewis will wash the cups. That's what you
pay her for, for heaven's sake.'

The next couple of days dragged.

Pleading pressure of work, Maggie managed to avoid her
weekly lunch date with Jackie, although actually she was
coping fairly well. No thanks to her sister, she conceded
drily on Saturday evening. For all her boast about not being
useless, Jackie hadn't been near the office while Maggie
was away. The information Jackie had dropped so casually
had been obtained from Lucy, Maggie's assistant, by
phone. It was thanks to Lucy, and no one else, that there
wasn't a heap of files on Maggie's desk.

Even so, Maggie was tired as she drove home that evening. It wasn't so much a physical tiredness as a mental
one, and the fact that she was going back to an empty house
again weighed heavily on her mind. What if Lindsey de-

cided she wanted to stay with her father? she mused unhappily. What if she decided to finish her education at the school that Tim Fitzgerald attended?

It could happen.

Maggie shuddered at the thought, but it wouldn't go away. What kind of a life would be left to her, with only her work to look forward to? How could she maintain any kind of relationship with her daughter if she was so far away?

Of course, Jackie would say she was a fool to worry. That she should be grateful if Neil chose to take the problem of Lindsey's future out of her hands. But she loved her daughter; for all her faults, she loved her dearly. She loved Neil, too, but he was already lost to her.

It was futile now to wish she had compromised and opened a shop in Newcastle instead of London. If she hadn't been so sure Neil would change his mind, she'd never have risked them living apart. Neil hadn't wanted her to work, yet he had been prepared to finance her. How selfish she had been not to consider his feelings as well as her own.

It would be easy to put some of the blame onto Jackie, easy to console herself with the thought that without her sister's encouragement she would never have made a stand. But Jackie wasn't to blame for her belligerence. She'd wanted her own way, and now she was paying the price.

For once, no one was parked in front of her house, and she slotted the little Peugeot into the space without too much effort. She'd brought a couple of files home with her, and she was planning to spend the evening checking Lucy's figures. Not quite the way she would have chosen to spend a Saturday evening, but it was better than sitting worrying about the future.

It was when she stepped into the hall and discovered the alarm wasn't activated that a feeling of apprehension gripped her. Oh, God, she thought uneasily, did that mean someone was in the house?

She had switched the hall light on as she'd come in, and now she moistened her dry lips and moved to the foot of the stairs. 'Lindsey?' she called, her voice thin and anxious. Surely her daughter wasn't with Mike Reynolds again?

But no. Lindsey was in Northumberland. And wouldn't she have let her mother know if she was coming back? A thought occurred to her: perhaps Mike Reynolds had a key to the house too. He might be waiting for her now to exact his revenge...

'Hello, Maggie.'

Her jaw sagged. It wasn't Mike Reynolds but Neil, standing at the top of the stairs.

'I hope you don't mind. I borrowed Lindsey's keys,' he added quietly. 'I didn't want to startle you, but I was afraid if I waited until you got home you wouldn't let me in.'

Maggie felt dizzy suddenly, and she remembered she hadn't had anything to eat since that morning. And then only half a slice of toast, washed down with several cups of coffee. In fact, since she'd come back, she hadn't had much appetite at all.

'Where's Lindsey?' she asked, when the swimminess in her head abated somewhat. All she could think was that Neil had come here to tell her Lindsey wasn't coming back, and although it was what she had half anticipated that didn't make it any easier to take.

'Why don't you come upstairs, and we'll have a drink?' suggested Neil, without answering her. 'You look tired, Maggie. Isn't Jackie pulling her weight?'

And if she's not, what are you going to do about it? thought Maggie wearily. She caught her lower lip between her teeth. There was no point in giving him that satisfaction too.

Deciding she might as well get it over with, she started up the stairs, dropping her overcoat over the banister as she went. Her business suit was creased, but Neil hadn't come here to look at her. Except, perhaps, with pity, she reflected bitterly.

For once the warm ambience of her sitting room didn't soothe her. The sight of her ex-husband standing squarely on the Turkish rug before the fireplace filled her with alarm. In a black leather jacket and matching denims, he looked strong and invincible, the day's growth of stubble on his chin only adding to his powerful façade.

'Whisky?' he asked as she came into the room, and she saw the empty glass in his hand. Evidently he'd been helping himself to a drink while he'd been waiting for her, and although it was small-minded she found herself resenting it.

'No, thanks,' she said, the fact that she hadn't eaten all day preventing her from accepting the false courage the alcohol might have given her. It was hard enough to face this interview as it was. She needed a clear head when he got to the point of his visit. 'But don't let me stop you from having another.'

Neil's lips twisted. 'You begrudge me a drink?'

'I didn't say that.'

'You didn't have to.' He set his glass behind him on the mock-Georgian mantel that framed the marble hearth. 'Which doesn't augur well for why I came. Perhaps I should have waited until tomorrow.'

'Perhaps you should.' Maggie unbuttoned the jacket of her suit, and bracketed her throat with a nervous hand. 'I gather, as she isn't here, that Lindsey isn't with you.'

'No.' Neil's lips were compressed now. 'No, as you've probably guessed, she's decided she wants to spend a little time at Haversham. In the circumstances, I didn't think you would object.'

Maggie took a breath. 'A little time?' She lifted a wary shoulder. 'What does that mean?'

'It means—a little time,' said Neil evenly. 'I thought—initially—until Easter. We can probably review the situation then.'

'Easter!'

Maggie managed to sound as if she was considering it, but in fact she was feeling an enormous sense of relief. She'd been expecting Neil to tell her that Lindsey wasn't coming back at all. Easter was only a couple of months away.

'I know you're going to say her education will suffer,' Neil went on, before she could comment further. ''But what's a little time out if it will make her happy? I'd rather she wasn't forced to choose between us.'

Maggie held up her head. 'All right.'

Neil blinked. 'You agree?'

'Well, I can see that she's more likely to get over her infatuation for Mike Reynolds in another place,' said Maggie carefully. 'Um—how is she? Have you talked to her?'

'At length,' said Neil, somewhat flatly, raking a restless hand through his hair. 'After Luke's outburst, I had to tell her how easy it had been for Mike to falsify the royalties. When you trust someone, you don't expect them to let you down.'

Maggie stiffened. 'Am I supposed to respond to that?'

Neil sighed. 'No.'

'But it was directed at me, wasn't it?'

'No, it wasn't.' He thrust his hands into the pockets of his jacket and stared down at the toes of his boots. 'As a matter of fact, I was trying to get around to asking you if you'd like to spend a couple of weeks at Haversham yourself. I know it's not your favourite place, and if you turn me down I'll have to live with it. But—' he lifted his head and looked at her, his narrowed eyes dark and compelling '—I think we could stand to look at our relationship again. Since you came back to London, I've been thinking about little else.'

CHAPTER FIFTEEN

'OH?'

Maggie's throat was dry, and although she desperately wanted to believe that Neil had come to this position of his own accord snippets of the conversation he had had with Lindsey kept coming back into her head.

'Have you talked to her?'

'At length.'

But what about?

'Yes,' Neil continued now, holding her uncertain gaze with his. 'That afternoon in the stables at Haversham, when you said you'd never had an affair with Massey...' He paused. 'Well, whether you did or not, it doesn't matter. Since—since seeing you again, since being with you again, I've realised I still want you in my life.'

Maggie's breath caught in her throat. 'You want me in your life?'

'Yes.'

'Just like that?'

'I don't know what that means,' said Neil heavily. 'I only know I need you. Perhaps it's a sign that I'm getting old. Whatever, I can't waste any more time wishing for miracles.' He sighed. 'Well? What do you say?'

Maggie blew out a trembling breath. 'What—what did Lindsey tell you?' she demanded unsteadily. 'What did she say to bring about this sudden change of heart?' She swallowed. 'She didn't happen to explain what really happened between me and Oliver Massey, did she? Something you could latch onto to redeem your sudden desire to have sex with me?'

'It's not a sudden desire to have sex,' he responded

harshly, his skin darkening with heat. 'For God's sake, Maggie, do you think I'd discuss my feelings for you with our daughter? Or ask her to adjudicate over something that should never have happened?'

'Oh, I agree, it should never have happened,' said Maggie, forcing herself to turn away from him. 'But you can't expect me to believe that you've suddenly decided to listen to my side of the story without any cause.'

'No, that's right.' His response startled her. 'I haven't decided to listen to your side of the story. I don't want to hear your side of the story. I didn't want to hear it when it happened, and I don't want to hear it now.'

Maggie's head swung round. 'Then why——?'

'Haven't you been listening to me?' Neil was breathing unevenly. 'I told you. It was when you started talking about Massey that I realised he didn't matter. My—my feelings for you haven't changed. As much as I might have wanted them to, they haven't. Seeing you again was like—like a revelation. Why the hell do you think I followed you down here?'

Maggie stared at him. 'I thought you were concerned about Lindsey.'

'I was.'

'So...?'

'Oh, Maggie, don't be so obtuse. You know very well that I could have spoken to Lindsey without involving you.' He sighed. 'I didn't have to invite you to Haversham. I think I could have persuaded Lindsey to come on her own.'

Maggie swallowed. He was probably right. The relationship she had had with her daughter at that time would hardly have been conducive to changing her mind. But she still didn't understand what he was saying. Or comprehend his desire not to learn the truth.

She shook her head, trying to make sense of his meaning. 'Are you saying you believe me now?'

'Believe you?' Neil sounded impatient, and she was sure it was just a supreme effort of will on his part that kept him where he was. She had the feeling he would have liked to shake some sense into her, but he was shrewd enough to know that violence would achieve nothing. 'Maggie, I'm saying it doesn't matter.'

She stiffened. 'So, even though you say you—you still have feelings for me—'

'I do.'

'—you don't believe I didn't have an affair with Oliver Massey?'

'God, Maggie—'

'Is that right?'

He closed his eyes against the insistence in her face. 'Does it matter?' he asked wearily. 'I've told you, I want you. Isn't that enough?'

Maggie sniffed. 'And you promise Lindsey said nothing about what I told her?'

'Yes.' Neil's eyes flicked open again, and there was a look of raw frustration on his face. 'God, Maggie, I'm through listening to anyone who thinks they have an input on our relationship. I guess Jackie thought she was doing you a favour at the time, but we know how that turned out.'

Maggie put a hand to her throat. 'Jackie?' she echoed faintly. 'What has Jackie to do with any of this?'

'It doesn't matter—'

'It does.' She turned and looked at him coldly. 'Are you saying it was Jackie who persuaded you to come here?'

'To come here?' His expression mirrored his incredulity, but Maggie was too unsure of herself to trust his words.

'Yes, to come here,' she said. 'I know she's been concerned about me since I got back.'

Neil's face twisted. 'The only person that woman has ever been concerned about is herself,' he retorted harshly. Then, as if realising he wouldn't help his case by criticising her sister, he held up a placating hand. 'For pity's sake, Maggie, I came here because I couldn't stay away.'

Maggie's lips trembled. 'Do you mean that?'

'How many more times?' he demanded, and, as if losing all control of his actions, he covered the space between them in a couple of strides. Cupping her face in his hands, he smoothed his thumbs over her eyebrows. 'I love you, Maggie. I may have hated you for what you did but I never stopped loving you.'

His mouth was soft, gentle, brushing against her lips with a tenderness he had never shown in the past, his hands sliding into her hair, holding her still beneath his sensual supplication until her hands, seeking a mooring on his hips, brought a less controlled response.

He kissed her now with a fierceness that exposed the need he'd spoken of before. Pulling her closer, her breasts flattening against his chest, hip to hip, thigh to thigh, trying to penetrate the barrier of their clothes. She could feel every taut muscle of his body straining towards her, smell the heat of his arousal mingling with the clean scent of his body.

Neil groaned as her arms slid around his waist, the sound, low in his throat, possessing a bone-tingling excitement. His hand slid down to find the swollen budding of her breast. The buttons of her shirt were soon parted, and his fingers slid inside her bra to find one engorged nipple, his thumb rubbing across it until she was weak with longing.

His kisses deepened, his tongue finding its way into her mouth and possessing it without restraint. 'I want you so much,' he whispered unsteadily, parting his legs to draw her nearer. 'I can't sleep nights for thinking of how hot and tight you felt around me. I want to be inside you now, inside you so deep, I lose what little sanity I have left.'

'Neil—'

'It's true,' he protested, hearing the slight trace of resistance that still lingered in the word. 'God, Maggie, don't make me wait any longer…'

She wanted to hold back. She still had questions she wanted answers to; but she had needs as well, and, as with him, the demands of the moment outweighed everything else. Besides, the urgent thrust of his hard body was unbearably appealing, and she was woman enough to know that any conversation they had now would only exacerbate an already explosive situation.

'My—my bedroom's upstairs,' she ventured huskily, and Neil drew back to cup her face once again.

'Show me,' he said, and before she could think of some

reason why she should change her mind Maggie started out the door.

Her bedroom was cool. Although she left the heating on during the day, it was at a reduced temperature, but even though her skin feathered with goose flesh she didn't feel the cold. The sight of Neil tearing off his jacket, unbuttoning his trousers, stripping off his shirt was enough to turn the blood to fire in her veins.

Her own jacket was easily discarded, but her fingers fumbled with the remaining buttons of her shirt, and as if unable to keep his hands off her any longer Neil came and disposed of the offending article himself. Then, removing her bra, he took a moment to cradle the sensitive fullness of her breasts, before moving on to her skirt.

When she was completely naked, he didn't immediately take her to the bed. Instead, he knelt before her, and pressed his face against the quivering junction of her legs. 'I love you,' he told her, against the moist curls that guarded her femininity. 'You're the only woman I've ever loved.'

Their lovemaking was swift and satisfying. By the time Neil had shed his jeans and boxers, Maggie was beyond any thought of restraint, and she wound her legs so tightly about his waist that the thickness of his erection penetrated deeper than ever before. They were so finely attuned to one another's needs that Neil held back from the ultimate act that would drive them both over the brink, prolonging the ecstasy, until Maggie's nails digging into his shoulders forced him to go on. He rose above her, meeting her gaze at the moment he swept them both away, and they shared the bliss of total fulfilment...

It was the sound of someone ringing the doorbell that awakened Maggie.

She opened her eyes with some reluctance to find Neil stirring beside her, and although she wanted nothing so much as to ignore it the sound just wouldn't go away.

'Who the hell is it?' muttered Neil as she turned on the lamp at her side of the bed. 'It's the middle of the night!'

Maggie's lips twitched. 'It's eight o'clock,' she corrected

him gently. And as the bell rang again she said, 'I'd better see who it is.'

'Well, get rid of them,' Neil told her huskily, bestowing a lingering kiss on the corner of her mouth. 'I haven't finished with you yet.'

Maggie couldn't resist it. 'Haven't you?' she asked teasingly, and Neil moved to imprison her beneath the undoubted strength of his body.

'You'd better believe it,' he breathed, brushing her eyelids with his lips. 'Tomorrow, I'm going to buy a special licence to prove it.'

Maggie cradled his face in her hands, her eyes wide with wonder. 'Do you mean it?'

'Would I lie about something like that?' he asked, his gaze dark and impassioned. Then, as the doorbell rang again, he growled, 'Oh, go and shut them up, for God's sake. I want to make love to my wife.'

Maggie's legs were trembling as she got out of bed, and, lingering only long enough to pull on a mauve silk wrapper, she sped swiftly down the two flights of stairs. Her thoughts were all of the things Neil had said, so that when she peered through the peephole and saw her sister waiting outside on the doorstep she was tempted to pretend she wasn't home after all. But she had been foolish enough to put on the light, and Jackie was evidently in no mood to be ignored.

'Open the door, Maggie,' she called impatiently. 'If I'd thought you'd be in the bath, I'd have phoned before I left home.'

Maggie unlocked the door and opened it a crack. 'In the bath?' she echoed uncomprehendingly, and Jackie, undeterred by her sister's reluctance to invite her in, brushed past her into the hall.

'Close the door, for goodness' sake!' she exclaimed. 'It's freezing out there. You'll catch your death.'

Maggie did as she was told, and endeavoured to gather the folds of her gown more closely about her. As her brain cleared, she began to see the advantages of maybe pretending she had been in the bath, after all. Her reconciliation with Neil was too fresh, too new, too fragile to expose to Jackie's cynical gaze, and she wanted to be absolutely certain that Neil meant what he said before running the risk of making a fool of herself again.

'So,' she said, trying to sound casual. 'To what do I owe this pleasure? You don't normally come round so late.'

'Eight o'clock's hardly late,' said Jackie, glancing up the stairs, and for an awful moment Maggie wondered if she knew Neil was here. 'Um—can we talk?' She grimaced. 'Not down here. It's too cold.'

Maggie hesitated. 'Well—is it important?' she asked, not wanting to invite her sister upstairs, and Jackie gave an impatient sigh.

'I'd hardly be here otherwise, would I?' she exclaimed irritably. Then, seeing that Maggie was still not convinced, she said, 'It's about Neil.'

'Neil?' Now Maggie's eyes were drawn upwards, but she hid their guilty message by gesturing towards the stairs. 'I suppose you'd better come up to the sitting room,' she added, not at all sure that what she was doing was terribly wise. 'As—as you say, I don't want to catch a chill.'

'No.'

But Jackie's agreement was scarcely gracious, and she preceded her sister up the stairs with an air of injured dignity. She evidently thought Maggie should have been more pleased to see her, and in normal circumstances she probably would have been. Though recently Maggie had begun to see her sister in a different light.

Fortunately, the lamps were still on in the sitting room, which seemed to confirm Jackie's supposition that she had been taking a bath. What Jackie would have said, had she known why her sister had left the room so precipitously, Maggie couldn't imagine. Or perhaps she could. She just didn't want to think about it now.

Closing the door without securing it, Maggie paused and regarded the other woman with an uplifted brow. 'What about Neil?' she asked, unable to think of anything Jackie might have to tell her, and apprehensive of hearing something she wouldn't like.

'Good heavens!' Jackie plumped herself down onto the sofa, and gave her sister an indignant look. 'It's obvious you don't entertain very often. You're supposed to offer a guest a drink.'

Maggie took a deep breath. 'You know where the drinks are,' she said. 'Help yourself. As you pointed out before, I was in the middle of—of having a bath.'

'Oh, well... If you're going to be like that...'

Jackie got up, as if to go, and, realising she would only regret it if she didn't listen to what she had to say, Maggie waved her back. 'G and T?' she asked shortly, tying the belt of her robe and treading barefoot across to the tray. 'With ice? Or lemon? Or both?'

'Just ice,' declared Jackie, sinking back onto the sofa with obvious satisfaction. 'Mmm,' she said, after she'd tasted her drink. 'This is nice, isn't it? We ought to spend more time together, you know.'

'Jackie!'

'Oh, all right.' Jackie took another mouthful of her gin and tonic, and then cradled the glass between her palms. 'I just thought I should tell you I've had a call from Lindsey. She says she's staying with her father for the time being.'

'I—Oh!' Maggie just managed to prevent herself from saying that she already knew that. 'I—wonder why she didn't ring me herself?'

'Well...' Jackie moistened her lips '...you know she and I have always been close, and I expect she didn't want to upset you. Particularly as Neil is thinking of getting married again.'

Maggie's jaw sagged. 'What?'

'I knew you'd be upset.' But Jackie didn't look as if she was concerned about it. 'You knew he was seeing that Braithwaite woman, didn't you? You told me so yourself. I must admit I was surprised that Lindsey has taken the news so calmly. Even though you and she have had your differences in the past, I'd have thought she owed you a little more loyalty than her father.'

Maggie stared at her. 'Lindsey told you her father is going to marry Nicola Braithwaite?'

She couldn't believe it. She *wouldn't*.

'Well, not in so many words.' Inadvertently, Jackie reassured her. 'She didn't have to. Maggie, when I heard Neil was getting married to someone else, I breathed a sigh of relief. I know what he thinks of me, and I've always been afraid he'd try and split us up. Whatever that bastard says, I've always had your well-being at heart.'

Maggie blinked. 'I know that.'

'Do you? Do you honestly?' Jackie stared at her so intently now that, despite herself, Maggie could feel the hot colour staining her cheeks. 'Then will you forgive me if I tell you that I lied about your relationship with Oliver Massey? I didn't tell you this at the time, but Neil did ring one evening when you were staying at the flat.'

Maggie caught her breath. 'At your flat?'

'Yes.' Jackie licked her lips. 'He—he was so abusive to me. I know I shouldn't have done it, but I said you were out with—with Oliver.'

'What you actually said was that Maggie was *living* with Massey,' remarked Neil from behind them, his voice as cold as ice. 'That they'd been having an affair for the past six months!'

Maggie gasped, and Jackie sprang to her feet, spilling the remains of her gin and tonic down the front of her expensive sheepskin coat. Neil stood propped against the door-jamb, wearing only his jeans, the button at his waist unfastened to reveal the dark hair that arrowed down to his navel.

'Neil!' Jackie's dismay was manifest. Then, with more venom, she demanded, 'What are you doing here?' She looked at Maggie's shocked face. 'How could you do this to me? Why didn't you tell me? My God, you weren't in the bath at all. You've been having sex with him!'

'My wife—my wife-to-be—and I were making love,' Neil corrected her mildly. Then, his expression softening as he looked at Maggie, he added, 'And you interrupted us.'

Jackie's face was contorted with hatred. 'I knew it,' she said. 'I knew you'd try to worm your way back into her affections.' She gave Maggie a filthy look. 'And you let him. Oh, Maggie, how could you?'

Maggie's lips parted. 'I love him, Jackie. I always did.'

'You were infatuated with him,' retorted Jackie, dabbing

at her coat with an agitated hand. 'You were never happy, not really. You always deserved something better, someone better.'

'So long as it wasn't me, is that it?' suggested Neil, his mouth thin and dangerous. 'What's wrong, Jackie? Did you resent your sister's happiness? Did you resent the fact that she could hang onto her man, whereas yours was always looking elsewhere for the warmth he couldn't find at home?'

'Shut up!'

'No, why should I? You've had it all your own way long enough. Why don't you tell Maggie the real truth—that you were jealous of her? That splitting us up wasn't working, so you decided to deliver the *coup de grâce*!'

'I don't know what you're talking about.' Jackie turned to Maggie, as if for support, but Maggie quickly moved to Neil's side. The words he'd used, the things he'd said, the actions he'd accused Jackie of were just now penetrating her dazed senses, and she stared at her sister as if she'd never seen her before.

'I think you'd better go,' she said as Neil's arm came around her, drawing her securely against his hip. She slid her arm around his waist, feeling the reassuring warmth of his skin beneath her fingers. 'As you can see, Lindsey was right; Neil is getting married again. But not to Nicola Braithwaite. To me!'

'And I suppose you're going to tell me he believes that pathetic story you told about Oliver Massey forcing you to have sex with him, aren't you?' demanded Jackie disgustedly. 'My God!'

'You know,' said Neil softly, but with an undertone of menace in his voice, 'if that had mattered to me before—and it didn't—you'd have just convinced me to believe her.' His lips curled. 'Poor Jackie! It looks like you struck out on all counts.'

'I didn't ring Aunt Jackie; she rang me,' Lindsey told them the following afternoon, when, after spending the night at Prince's Crescent, Neil had driven Maggie back to

Northumberland. 'She said you'd given her the number, Mum, and she was just calling to see how I was feeling. Apparently you'd told her about Daddy throwing Mike out.'

'Well, I did,' said Maggie doubtfully. 'But I didn't give her the number. Though I expect she could have got it from Lucy. That's my secretary,' she added for Neil's benefit. 'She would think there was no reason why Jackie shouldn't be told.'

Neil nodded, and, as if just realising that her mother had come back with her father, Lindsey quirked an enquiring brow. 'Is that all you have to say?'

'Well…' Maggie hesitated, and then, after exchanging a glance with Neil, she moved closer to the fire. 'Jackie also said that you'd told her that your father was thinking of getting married again.'

'Did she?' Now it was Lindsey's turn to look discomfited, and Maggie was amused at the way the girl's eyes moved to her father for guidance. 'Well, perhaps that was just—wishful thinking.' She grimaced. 'Did you have a good trip?'

Maggie hid her amusement. 'But why would you tell Jackie something like that?' she persisted, and Neil took the initiative and flung himself onto one of the sofas.

'I'm not sure your mother appreciated your eagerness to acquire a stepmother,' he remarked idly. 'I know she's not fond of Nicola, and I had thought that you felt the same.'

'Nicola!' Lindsey stared at each of them in turn, but although Neil managed to keep a straight face Maggie's gulp of laughter gave the game away. 'You—you—' she began, only to have her father say, 'Careful!' and then she flung herself into her mother's arms and waltzed her round the floor.

It was some moments before order returned, Lindsey insisting that Neil join in the celebrations, and it was only when Luke appeared in the doorway that they were forced to settle down.

'Does this mean what I hope it means?' he exclaimed, looking at Neil optimistically. 'Oh, man, I couldn't be more delighted. Maggie, you're back where you belong.'

'Not so fast,' said Neil soberly, though he kept both his women close to him. 'Maggie and I haven't worked out the details yet. We may be moving back to town.'

'I don't think so,' said Maggie quickly, before Luke's expression had time to languish. 'As far as I'm concerned, my home's with you and Lindsey. Wherever that may be.'

'You mean we might live here?'

Maggie wasn't sure what she could hear in her daughter's voice, and her tone was cautious as she confirmed her words. 'But, if you want to stay in London, you could board through the week, if you want. Or I could have a word with Mrs Lewis. I'm sure something could be arranged.'

'No.' Lindsey was very definite suddenly. 'If it means we'll be together, then Haversham is good enough for me.' She coloured at her father's offended look, and punched him gently in the midriff. 'You know what I mean,' she told him fiercely. 'I can wait until I go to college to live on my own.'

'There's still your mother's business,' pointed out Neil steadily. 'I don't want Jackie accusing me of stifling her ambition again.'

'She won't.' Maggie was equally certain. 'And, like Lindsey, this is my home too.'

'Well, you could always open a shop in Newcastle,' said Luke, voicing something Maggie had considered only days before...before she'd known that Neil still loved her.

'I could,' she agreed happily. 'But for now Lucy can take control. In fact, I might make her a director. That way, she'd have a vested interest in making the business a success.'

Neil's fingers tightened on her waist, but only she was aware of it. 'You won't regret it,' he said huskily, and Luke beckoned to Lindsey.

'I think there's some champagne in the cellar,' he said softly. 'Let's you and I go and look for it, while your father shows your mother where she's going to sleep.'

'Where she's going to sleep?' echoed Lindsey uncomprehendingly, and then seemed to realise what Luke was really saying.

'Oh—yes,' she muttered, scuttling towards him. 'Some champagne! That sounds really good.'

'What would we do without Luke?' murmured Neil as their footsteps echoed across the hall. 'I'm sure he's going to come in very handy in the days ahead.'

'Oh? Why?' asked Maggie innocently as he pulled her into his arms.

'Children can be very lovable but also very nosy, when they're as old as our daughter,' replied Neil huskily, nuzzling her neck. 'It's just as well we're getting married again in a day or two. A honeymoon alone sounds much more fun...'

HARLEQUIN PRESENTS®

Don't miss these fun-filled romances that feature
fantastic men who *eventually* make fabulous fathers.
Ready or not...

Watch for:
June 1997—FINN'S TWINS! (#1890)
by Anne McAllister
July 1997—THE DADDY DEAL (#1897)
by Kathleen O'Brien

FROM HERE TO PATERNITY—
men who find their way to fatherhood
by fair means, by foul, or even by default!

Available wherever Harlequin books are sold.